First published in Great Britain in 2024 by
Peirene Press Ltd
The Studio
10 Palace Yard Mews
Bath BA1 2NH

First published in German as *Halbschwimmer*
Copyright © Katja Oskamp 2003. All rights reserved.

This translation © Jo Heinrich 2024

Katja Oskamp asserts her moral right to be identified as the author of this work in accordance with the Copyright, Designs and Patents Act 1988.

All rights reserved. No part of this publication may be reproduced or transmitted in any form or by any means, electronic or mechanical, including photocopy, recording or any information storage and retrieval system, without permission in writing from the publisher.

ISBN 978-1-916806-00-9

This book is a work of fiction. Names, characters, businesses, organizations, places and events are either the product of the author's imagination or used fictitiously. Any resemblance to actual persons, living or dead, events or locales is entirely coincidental.

The translation of this work was supported
by a grant from the Goethe-Institut.

GOETHE-INSTITUT

Designed by Orlando Lloyd
Printed and bound in the U.K. by Clays Ltd, Elcograf S.p.A.

HALF SWIMMER

Katja Oskamp

Translated from the German
by Jo Heinrich

PEIRENE

Halbschwimmer
[noun]

Half Swimmer. A German term for one who has recently learned to swim but hasn't yet mastered the technique.

Rolf and Hopsi	1
Half Swimmer	13
Herr O	21
The Letter	37
Ruckedigu	51
What Custom Strictly Divided	73
Seventy-two Steps	91
Cut	115
Back on Speaking Terms	127

ROLF AND HOPSI

When I was a child, I had a hamster called Rolf. My parents bought him because I had to make do without any siblings. Rolf would sit under a pile of wood shavings in a glass enclosure by the door. He mostly slept; sometimes he'd eat something. He never used his wheel. The best thing about Rolf was the way he could get my father to throw himself on the floor and stick his head under the cupboard. Apart from that, Rolf was a disappointment and he soon died.

Then I got two black dwarf rabbits: Hopsi One and Hopsi Two. The rabbit hutch was on the balcony, clear varnish peeling from its wooden panels. I only cleaned the hutch when my father forced me to. I'd bring the dwarf rabbits into the living room for hours every afternoon to sit them on the carpet in front of me and pull their back legs: it was called playing wheelbarrows, a well-known children's game.

Compared to the unimaginative repetition of Hopsi as the rabbits' names, I think the hamster's name, Rolf, was quite original. I named him after the father of the family next door, the Wiedemeyers, who were friends of ours. The Wiedemeyers were Uncle Rolf, Auntie Elke and the children, Jan and Fanny. Uncle Rolf wasn't very happy when I told him my hamster's name. Actually, I should have seen that as a sign. I didn't think to ask whether he disliked his name so much that he didn't want it copied, or if his name was too good to be wasted on a hamster.

*

I push the packet of cigarettes behind the radiator halfway up the stairs. Somewhere that stupid is the perfect hiding place. Sometimes I wonder if later, when I'm a grown-up and my father's finished with parenting, I ought to tell him that every morning he used to walk past the cigarettes he'd tried in vain to find in my things the night before.

I climb the last eleven steps to the third floor. The door to my parents' flat is hidden in a deep alcove off to the left. They've always said it's a privilege 'not to be on show', but even now I have a residual fear of turning off into the unknown: there might be someone lurking by the lift or behind the rubbish chute. The Wiedemeyers' door is on the right. I can make it out by the little orange glow over the light switch – I don't need to turn it on. Two fingers' breadth below the light switch there's the doorbell with the words 'Dr Wiedemeyer & Family' stamped in white letters on a black plastic strip. My father wrote our surname by hand on the white section next to our doorbell, but it almost looks as though it's printed. We don't have a label maker like that. And we have a completely different sort of bell. When you press it, there's a continuous buzzing sound – you wouldn't really call it ringing. Sometimes the button gets stuck. When my mother's stressed, the button sticking can be the thing that sends her over the edge. My father tries to lever the button free again with the potato peeler, and meanwhile, anyone passing by can get a good look at my raging mother through the open door. Over the years our bell has become quieter and quieter, maybe from so much unintentional prolonged use. I don't know why my parents don't do something about it. They probably think it's not worth the trouble: it's not often that anyone other than the Wiedemeyers rings our doorbell.

The Wiedemeyers' bell makes a happy bing-bong sound. Recently I've been specializing in outsmarting their bell and I can now make it sound as hoarse and frail as ours. The trick is to stifle the bing and only let the bong happen; with the bing missing it sounds as if it's been strangled. You shouldn't, under any circumstances, press the button head-on with your thumb. Instead, you need to tap the button at an angle on its edge, not very hard, but of course not so gently that it doesn't make a sound at all. It's not just about the technique: it's also your inner mindset. If I picture myself as humble or apathetic, that's when I manage the tortured bell sound best. Just as Auntie Elke presses our button twice to let us know she's in a good mood, I can always be counted on to half-ring the Wiedemeyers' bell, and some days even ring it just a third or a quarter. That's how they know it's me.

The hallway's dark. I manage a quarter-ring, but it still seems too loud for this time of night. I quickly make the kind of face a scared child would make. Before I know it, I'm standing in front of Uncle Rolf, and he's standing in front of me in his pyjamas. He looks as if he's pleased. Come in, he says. It's not the first time.

'Are you watching TV?'

'Not really, it's just on.'

Everyone's asleep already – they've got to be up and out early. Only Uncle Rolf has a nightlife after ten. He pushes aside the blanket he must have had over him, and we sit down on the leather sofa. There are books lying around everywhere, and there's that magazine with the beautiful naked women; I think the Wiedemeyers have a subscription to it.

'Did you go to your dancing lessons again?'

'Well, you know I go every Thursday.'

'Was it good?'

'No, it was boring.'

Sometimes he's just so happy to see me. That's when Uncle Rolf takes my head in his hands and ruffles my hair and ears and everything. He's also the only one who's always said that the thing about my fat thighs is nonsense, that I should stop moaning because they're fine the way they are. Uncle Rolf laughs more than anyone else. He used to throw me over his shoulder, whirl me around and pinch my thighs until I couldn't help but scream with laughter. Once we accidentally hit a tomato plant's stake and I bled. I still have the scar.

'Come here.'

I slide over and curl my legs up beside me. Uncle Rolf's skin has large pores and is always covered with a fine glossy film; it's greasy skin, and his face gives off a certain smell if you get really close to it. In our family, no one has greasy skin. My skin, for example, is so dry it cracks in some places in winter if I don't put cream on it all the time. It would be good to mix my skin with Uncle Rolf's, then our skin type would be 'combination'.

'Have you got any chocolate?'

Uncle Rolf laughs again and reaches behind the sofa for the porcelain bowl, which Auntie Elke always keeps well stocked with bubbly chocolate and pralines.

When we were talking in his study a few weeks ago, he stroked my head and said, 'Wow, you're too clever by half!' Unfortunately, I can't remember what clever thing I'd said, but I want his hands to stroke me again. They're warm, soft and clean: proper doctor's hands.

The chocolate melts in my mouth. His fingertips touch my ribs and brush somewhere near my breast. He makes sure it's never completely in his hand. I take a deep breath, so that my breast reaches his hand. Boys can be so annoying, with their clumsy tongues. It's Uncle Rolf who makes me happy. I can't help pressing myself against him, holding him tight, and I know how it'll go next. I feel a little shudder, and Uncle Rolf takes my head in his hands, ruffles my hair again and pushes me up off the sofa.

'Off you go now, back home to bed.'

He walks me past the bedrooms, where Auntie Elke and the children are sleeping, to the front door. I give him a big smile as I say goodbye; I can't think of anything better to do. Then I stand there in the dark, my cheeks glowing.

The Wiedemeyers are sitting in their usual places in my parents' lounge. My mother's decided to 'clear the air' today. I've made a cosy nest out of my bedding and I'm listening to them fight it out in the living room. But I don't know whose side I'm on.

My mother talks to the Wiedemeyers in a forceful tone and then shouts that this friendship has not been mutual for a long time, that she's tired of being taken advantage of and that Auntie Elke should stop giving her used lipsticks. Uncle Rolf laughs from time to time and interrupts my mother's outburst with cheeky comments. Auntie Elke sobs and says that she and Uncle Rolf don't deserve this, but no one responds to her. I can't hear my father – I assume he's topping up everyone's glasses.

I wonder if the Wiedemeyers get upset with us behind closed doors, too, or if they're really surprised by this attack on them. In all probability the friendship's over after this. But how's it going to go with me and Uncle Rolf now? I can't just ring the enemy's doorbell.

It's two o'clock. Time has gone by very quickly. I'm still sitting in my bed, listening, but now I'm fed up with the row in there. I can't have a lie-in tomorrow: I've got to be at the bus station at six. Our class agreed to wash buses for the entire Sunday – it's what the Free German Youth call the 'peace shift'. I lie down and try to sleep. I can hear a low murmur from the hallway and the front door slams. The men are drunk, for sure, maybe even the women. My parents' bed creaks briefly, and then there's silence.

Then, suddenly, the doorbell's ringing and ringing, and there's banging at the door. I must have gone to sleep after all. Auntie Elke's beside herself.

'Rolf! Rolf's lying in the hallway like a corpse, he's foaming at the mouth!'

I find it hard to stay in my room: I'd love to see Uncle Rolf lying there like that. My father calls the doctor, but by the time he arrives, Uncle Rolf's back on his feet again.

'Too much alcohol and excitement can affect the circulation, it happens with choleric types,' the doctor says before disappearing again. The doors stay open a while longer. The timed light in the hallway keeps turning itself off, over and over again. By the time they all go to bed, it's five o'clock, and I get up.

'I'll take you.'

'Don't you want to go to bed?'

'Did you get any sleep?'

'No.'

My father cleans his teeth after I've done mine and takes two apples from the kitchen. He puts his key in the lock to make sure the door closes quietly. I stop halfway down the stairs. There's bound to be a break on the peace shift and then we'll have a smoke. I reach behind the radiator and take out the packet of cigarettes. My father gives me a slap on the back of the head with one hand, an apple with the other, and grins.

The air outside is mild. It's a twenty-minute walk to the bus station, and there aren't any buses that early, especially not on a Sunday. They probably need to be washed first.

At school we learn and repeat the sentence 'War is the continuation of politics by military means,' which makes such an impression on me that I try to apply it to my life. I rewrite the sentence for the new situation at home: 'Children are the continuation of their parents by younger means.' I never hang around with Jan and Fanny any more. When I meet them in the hallway, they're always going somewhere in a hurry. The thought of them ringing my doorbell again is unimaginable. My parents say it would have happened sooner or later anyway.

I'm not that sorry about Jan: I could never understand why Uncle Rolf had such a stupid son. But with Fanny the situation's more complicated. As well as the queen-in-jail game, where we take turns locking each other in the loo, turning off the lights and standing outside demanding pledges to do better or face even harsher punishments, we've also made up a game where we say a word over and over again in quick succession until it loses all meaning and becomes nothing but a strange, monotonous tune – we have a lot of fun making ourselves lightheaded like that. Although, actually, we haven't played those games for ages.

Instead, I turn to school, in other words to Herr Bading, my class tutor and maths teacher. I have his student advice sessions all to myself; after all, none of the others choose to go to them. Herr Bading's first name is Peter, he has two grown-up children and he's divorced. Now he lives with another woman, but he's not married to her. At the weekends he always goes to his little lakeside cabin. Sometimes Herr Bading tries to talk to me about my problems with maths, physics and chemistry, but I've already told him that these things hold only a very limited interest for me and that they need to be seen in a wider context. After a while, we spend the time philosophizing about life and he tells me about something from his. At the end, when I leave, he often shakes my hand, and it always feels as if it's still covered in chalk. Once he even patted me on the back. It felt empowering somehow, but I was afraid I'd be walking around school with a white handprint on my back, so I put my coat on straight away. I can imagine Herr Bading might not be entirely comfortable with me, because he has to be on his guard as a teacher, but he also enjoys our time together. I can't be bothered with all that. I keep thinking of questions to ask him at the next student advice session; and after each one, I dream about Herr Bading taking me to his cabin and us swimming in the lake together, and about getting a better mark in maths, too.

*

In my letter to Uncle Rolf I write that, after six years, I've split up with my boyfriend Karl because of his age. I also write that I can't help looking up at the Wiedemeyers' balcony when I visit my parents, and that it would be nice to see him again.

Weeks go by, and then Uncle Rolf rings me. He cheerfully tells me how pleased he was to receive such a long and lovely letter from me, especially these days when bills are all that ever comes through the letterbox. He's well but he has a lot on his plate, so it's not convenient to meet at the moment. He'd like to see me, of course, maybe in two or three weeks when things have calmed down – he'll definitely get in touch again then.

I put the receiver down and feel stupid. My mother used to say that girls should play hard to get. I just can't; it's not in my nature. Uncle Rolf doesn't ring back, not after a month, not after two months. He's put me on hold until nevermore.

It's the first time I've visited my parents since Paula was born. I've got her in a sling under my coat. As I reach the corner, I'm already looking up at the balcony: nothing, as always. A car pulls up by the entrance. Uncle Rolf is behind the wheel, reaching across to open the passenger door, and beckoning me in. With Paula on my front, I can hardly sit down, and I definitely can't sink into the car seat without crushing her, so I struggle into an inclined position with my hips forward, tucking my head in and pulling the door closed.

'You look so different.'

As I say this, I remember my recent weight gain and I'm

expecting Rolf to respond with something equally uncharitable. But he just laughs, revealing a full set of unfamiliar teeth.

'How are things?'

I'm grateful to him for steering the conversation away from our ages and how much we've changed. I laugh back, as best I can, and beckon with a nod to Paula.

'See for yourself.'

Rolf peeks at the bundle on my front, but apart from the ugly hospital hat and two fists, there's nothing to see.

'What's her name?'

'Hopsi.'

We both laugh then, and I'm so glad: glad I thought of saying that, glad Rolf's laying his hand on my neck and pressing his face against mine and glad we don't have to look at each other any more. We catch our breath together for a while, long enough for there to be a real chance of forgetting what I've just seen. And then I can smell his good, old skin again, and I'm overcome with a great weakness.

'Off you go now, go and see them.'

I pull myself together, throw open the passenger door and hear the car drive off. I don't want to go upstairs yet – I'm sweating buckets, and Paula's still asleep – so I go for a walk through the estate, and I realize I no longer have a clue what Uncle Rolf's always laughing about. Then I ring my parents' doorbell.

HALF SWIMMER

Dad's teaching me how to dive with my eyes open. He persuades me to try. Just give it a go, he says, and I do.

It's murky down there: the seabed's been churned up by all the floundering holidaymakers. Dad and I stare at one another, making faces. I can faintly hear my own laughter, but Dad can probably only see the bubbles. They rise up out of my mouth, and when I run out of bubbles, I rise up myself, gasping for air on the surface.

Before the line where sea meets sky, windsurfers are leaning backwards and forwards on their colourful triangles. On land, sandcastles are piling up, and families seem to live in them. Parasols. Cool bags. Inflatables. And children of all sizes, being noisy. It's holiday time by the Baltic Sea.

Dad comes swimming up to me with that look again: he's acting innocent. I change direction, trying to get away, but I can't swim any more: I'm just treading water, and even then I'm choking. I thrash around, but I can't get moving – I'll probably never be any more than a half swimmer, ever. My upper arms and belly are hurting, like they're cramping up. I thrash, splash and choke.

Dad comes up to me with calm, deliberate strokes, and he still has the strength to keep making that innocent expression. I stop struggling. Giving up feels like a relief. Next thing, he's baring his teeth, but he's not laughing: he clenches them like a sprinter reaching the finish line and, with his hand outstretched, he pushes my head underwater. I'm sinking and he's rising. I close my eyes. He goes for my wrist, and then takes hold of my ankle. I kick around, hitting out instinctively, and worm my head out of his grasp. Then he pushes me deep down by the shoulder; no matter what I do, he always manages to latch on to me somewhere. My knee slams against something hard and he stops. He's stopped! I float up to the surface, coughing, wheezing and spluttering. Fresh air! Normally he stops earlier. My lungs are pumping. My heart's racing. Then he's next to me, out of breath, snorting like an angry billy goat. His bottom lip is bleeding. My eyes are burning from the salt water. Our teeth are chattering; he clamps his shut while I let mine go on rattling.

'You're bleeding,' I say.

'Really?' he says, running his tongue over his wound, 'Come on, let's get out.'

He turns away from me and shakes the water from his hair; the muscles in his thighs are bulging as he wades through the waves.

'I'll keep practising,' I shout. But my voice is too weak from all the air trying to get in and out.

There are no fish in the water, only human legs moving around in slow motion on the seabed, and slack jellyfish caught up in every swirl. I need to see them, those limp blobs, through the murky water. I keep my eyes wide open until grains of sand dig into my retinas and the salt blinds me, and then up I go. I gasp for air!

I wake up. My nightie's sticking to my skin, my eyes are crusty. There's a constant squeaking and creaking; that's what woke me up, not the heat, or the sun. It's quite regular, like the ticking of my alarm clock, at second intervals. Half past eight. Why is my bedroom door open?

I kick my covers to the foot of the bed and slowly roll to the edge to begin my descent. I don't want to make a sound and there's no need to rush it: I have plenty of time and strong muscles to hold me. I come to a halt after landing on all fours on the carpet.

The squeaking and creaking is still going, just as fast, just as loud. No one else seems to have noticed it. Time to go and see what it is. The walls are thin here in the holiday apartment, and nothing is far away. Every hand I lay down and every knee I let drop takes me silently out of the room. I look round the corner through the doorway and stop. My parents' bed has come into view!

I cautiously lower my forearms onto the hallway carpet, head down close to the ground, where no one would expect to find me. Most of me is out of sight, but my bottom's sticking up. My back is so arched the toddlers here could slide down it into their baby pool. So I shift my weight forward until my belly is on the carpet; my forearms will have to stay where they are, squashing into my chest. I can bear the pain, it's nothing.

All I can see is Dad's shoulder blades. A few black tufts are bobbing in white, choppy waves – that must be Mum's head. Further along, two pointy knees are sticking out of the foam at right angles. Two shark fins! They're after Dad, and they're keeping up with him. Focus, Dad, gather your strength. They're closing in! Dad's coming up to the surface every few breaths, gasping for air, with his head to the side and his eyes screwed up, then pressing his cheek back into the pillow, his hair dishevelled and stuck down with sweat. Don't lose your rhythm now! A hundred-metre crawl, your strongest discipline. Keep going, Dad, keep going!

There's a strong swell; breakers made of duvet. The sea whips against the bedroom wall. I can't see any arms reaching out: Mum must have drowned already. It's just the two triangles there, dangerously still, and Dad, who might still make it. He's starting the final spurt. The squeaking and creaking becomes a clatter and a gallop. There's no going back.

I push my bottom up again so I can get back to safety. To spare me and Dad the sight of each other. It's time to go. The toddler slide starts inching backward. Just don't panic, don't bump into anything, don't knock anything over. Dad hasn't crossed the finish line yet. I turn into my room; going backward is harder than going forward.

My little toenail snags on the carpet. It hurts. Keep still! It feels as if my toe's the weak point from which all my skin will be stripped off, over both my ears. I don't think they've heard a thing over there – or if Dad has, maybe it'll spur him on. I gently lift myself onto the bed. Twenty-seven minutes to nine. I'm safe. I'm exhausted.

I pull the covers over me, all the way over my head. I leave a small gap for breathing through, and for listening. The squeaking and creaking dies down, the rhythm's gone. Quiet. Finished. Done. No more sound, not a breath. No one says a thing. Not a word. Nothing.

Dad clears his throat. There's a squeak, once, then a creak, once. He's getting up now. I can't keep my eyes closed.

She's lying next to me in the sandcastle, flat and smooth like an eel, apart from one knee, which she's bent a little. Her face is covered with a magazine. Mum is brown all over, from head to toe; only her nipples, her belly button and her black pubic hair break the flow. Mum wants to get even browner, even more tanned. She rubs in suntan oil several times a day while we're on holiday. It makes her skin shiny, almost golden.

I sit with my legs drawn up and my back slouched over, the heat beating down on it. I've got sunburn, and I'm starting to peel.

I scratch open a blister at the base of my shin with a fingernail. When the milky grey skin comes loose, I use my thumbnail too and gently pull on the scrap until it tears off raggedly. Then I scratch open the next blister. Soon there are no more left on my shin – I've got to the end of them.

I turn to my shoulder, which gives better results. I pull off bigger scraps. They've even covered my pores, moles and little scars. They're not smooth at all: an endless pattern is imprinted on each fragment of skin, a tangled web of a thousand lines. Every layer I free myself from bears the same traces. I can shed my skin as often as I want. I let the scraps flutter like parchment in the sea breeze before my fingertips release them and they fly away. They get caught in the sandcastle's turrets and stick to the granular sand; only a few make it past them. I want to pull off huge pieces – great big pockets like the bubbles other people blow from gum. If I'm really careful, the very biggest ones make a noise like the lovely sound you get when you pull the skin off a salami, only much quieter.

I can't find any more to pull off on my shoulder. I'll have to be patient. I can't reach my back, no matter how much I contort myself. It's itchy. It's itchy from loose skin that wants to come off – I know it, I can see it, but I can't get to it.

'Stop picking,' Mum says.

'Peel my back,' I say.

She half-heartedly strokes it twice with the palm of her hand and accidentally scratches me with a sharp fingernail or one of her rings.

'Is it bleeding?' I ask.

'You'll never get a tan like that,' she says, covering her face with her magazine again. I cross my arms and start clawing into my shoulders. Take off the old skin, the dead stuff, take it all off!

When the water's evaporated, white salt remains on my skin and forms tracks like cracked earth. I lick it off my arm, licking salt like a goat.

Mum gets up. She doesn't like going in the water: just once a day and that's it. She takes a quick dip in the Baltic, spreads out her arms. A few frantic strokes with her neck outstretched and her mop of hair bobbing – it mustn't get wet – and she's out again. She dabs at her face with the towel: everything else has to air-dry so she doesn't spoil her golden artwork.

'Put some oil on and take your swimsuit off for once, don't be like that,' says Mum.

I go for a swim.

HERR O

It smelled weird: it smelled like something I'd never smelled before, a smell completely alien to me, which grew stronger the closer I got to our front door. I rummaged for my key among my schoolbooks. It didn't usually smell of anything in the hallway. But now it smelled a bit like Christmas, only better, or like a disco, only healthier. I liked the new scent. The door wasn't locked. Why was there someone home already? It was only a quarter to two.

I could hear faint music: Roger Whittaker, my mother's favourite record. I put my school bag down in the corridor and took off my shoes. The brown curtain was drawn. My father had removed the living room door to save space and replaced it with the curtain, just for decoration. We always left it open. But now it was drawn.

It smelled of cigarette smoke mixed with something else. I pushed the heavy fabric open a crack and slipped inside. Behind me, the curtain fell back without a sound.

I walked over the pale carpet in my socks and stopped in front of the lounge area.

'Hello,' I said.

My mother jumped up from the sofa where she'd been sitting cross-legged. She was barefoot. Her cheeks were flushed, her eyes shining. She looked impossibly beautiful. A man was sitting in the armchair opposite. I was looking at the back of his head; a bald spot was visible.

'Oh, it's you!' my mother said.

She knew when I came home from school and yet she was surprised. She hadn't heard me coming.

'Herr Oschlies is a colleague of mine,' she said.

My mother picked up the full ashtray and went to the bathroom. Herr Oschlies turned around in his chair. He was wearing glasses with brown frames. The thick lenses made his eyes look bigger. He stood up and held out his hand to me.

'Hello, Tanja,' he said.

His voice sounded deep and calm like Roger Whittaker's. I heard a flush: my mother had thrown the cigarette ends down the toilet.

'Pleased to meet you,' said Herr Oschlies.

I could tell Herr Oschlies was really nice. He wanted to see my mother had a good daughter. I made my 'mouse' face, in other words I smiled, but not a broad smile: a rather pointy one, with a wink.

On the coffee table there were two wide champagne glasses, almost drained, and an empty Rotkäppchen wine bottle. Next to it lay two Duett packets, one open and one screwed up. My first cigarette – I'd smoked it the previous month with my friend Nina – had been a Duett. My mother didn't smoke. Or at least she didn't smoke officially: she was a deputy headteacher which meant she had to be a role model. Unofficially, sometimes early in the mornings, she'd puff frantically on a cigarette to help her go to the loo. It never worked, but because of that one Duett she was plagued by a guilty conscience all day long, as if she'd smoked ten packets.

My mother came back from the bathroom. She had her deodorant in one hand. She pulled off the plastic cap with a pop, held the can high in the air and began spraying the scent, manically waving her arms to spread it around. Not only did she spray the lounge area, she sprayed every corner of the living room, walking in her bare feet from the dining table past the wall unit to the little telephone table. Then she pushed aside the brown curtain and carried on in the hall. Herr Oschlies and I stood in silence, shrouded in a cloud of Undine Green Apple.

It was time for him to be off: they'd discussed everything, Herr Oschlies said, half to me and half to himself. He pocketed the crumpled Duett packet, shook my hand again and went into the hall. I stayed where I was. So that was what I could smell: a mixture of Duetts and Undine Green Apple. My mother must have already been spraying the deodorant about before I'd got home. I hoped she hadn't been running around with the spray can after each little cigarette. I felt sorry for Herr Oschlies.

After saying goodbye to Herr Oschlies, my mother came back into the living room and flung open the balcony door. She put the pack of Duetts in the top drawer of the wall unit and took the champagne glasses and the empty bottle into the kitchen. Her face was glowing.

'Don't you have any homework?' she asked.

'What subjects does he teach?'

'Military education.'

Roger Whittaker was singing 'The Last Farewell'. I went to my room.

This time I could smell it as I was going up the stairs. It smelled good. I opened our door and closed it gently behind me. The brown curtain was drawn. Did my mother really think the curtain would hold back the clouds of smoke? Did she think the Undine Green Apple could cover the smell? As I was taking off my shoes, the door clicked behind me. I looked around, startled. My father was standing there, his briefcase in his hand. What was my father doing home from work so early?

'My meeting was postponed,' he said.

My father looked like a normal office worker. Although he was high up in the army, he always went to work in civilian clothes. I didn't know where he worked, or what he did there all day – for my mother and me, it was none of our business. But he left us in no doubt that he worked on very serious and highly dangerous things. That's why it was so important we didn't ask any questions: we had to keep something deadly secret, something not even we knew ourselves. He'd told me that if I was asked about his work at school, I should say he worked in military training. I went along with that. After all, it would have been embarrassing not to know what my father's job was at the age of thirteen.

He sniffed. I could hear him breathing in the Duett and Undine aroma through his nose. Just like I'd done a few weeks earlier, he was trying to identify the strange smell. I kept quiet.

My father pushed the brown curtain aside. I walked in behind him, in my socks. My mother jumped up from the sofa. She had that beautiful glow again.

'Eckart,' she said.

Herr Oschlies stood up.

'How are you, Günther?' my father asked.

The two men shook hands. A faint, meaningful grin was on their lips, as if they had something unspoken in common.

My mother reached for the ashtray. Papers – pages and pages – covered with printed charts, timetables and scribbles were piled up on the coffee table. Among them were two half-full coffee cups and two empty cognac glasses.

'We're working on some lesson plans,' my mother said.

There was a little elation in her face and something defiant in her voice. Maybe she was in the midst of a lesson plan frenzy.

'It smells like a brothel in here,' my father said.

'My God, Eckart, we'll be finished in a minute,' my mother said.

My father stared at the full ashtray in my mother's hand, then turned to me and said, 'Let's go for a jog.'

He gave my arm a shove and pushed me out of the room. I didn't object: I had the feeling there was one person too many in the apartment. But my father wanting to go jogging with me in the middle of the day was no less unnerving. Nothing like this had ever really happened before.

As an experienced jogging team, we found our pace straightaway. We ran in sync through the estate towards the hill in the Volkspark, which had been formed from rubble after the War. The park was overgrown with greenery: an oasis of fresh air in the middle of the city. My father had drummed it into me hundreds of times before that the most important thing with jogging was always to stay relaxed. His running style was extremely relaxed, so much so that his hands flapped up and down like two lifeless appendages hanging from his joints with every step. I preferred to make two fists.

'How do you know him?' I asked.

'Who, Herr O?'

I nodded. I couldn't speak, or I'd mess up my breathing and get a stitch.

Herr O. My father had a silly habit of abbreviating names; his address book was full of them. His abbreviation for me was Ta.

'He's responsible for military education in the district. He teaches at your school too,' he said.

My father explained that Herr O helped him recruit the next generation of military personnel; they visited classes together and looked for boys who were good professional soldier material.

So not only were my mother and Herr O colleagues – my father and Herr O seemed to be too.

'Is he in the army?'

I focused on the rhythm of my breathing. Inhale for two steps, exhale for three.

'Reserve lieutenant,' my father said.

'Is that higher than you?'

My father slapped his forehead.

'What am I?' my father asked.

'Major.'

'What was I before?'

'Captain.'

'And before that?'

I looked up at him and shrugged. How should I know? Besides, I'd just got a nasty stitch and I didn't want to talk any more. He gave me a slap on the back of the head and rolled his eyes in exasperation. And then my father listed all the ranks, from the very lowest to the highest, from private to general, three times and finally back down to the lowest again so I'd get it once and for all. When he started on the different epaulettes, I gave up listening. I was enjoying not having to talk any more and I focused on my breathing, happy I hadn't been born a boy.

It turned out that Herr O was small fry compared to my father. A teacher trained in maths and physics, he'd never been completely able to shake off his passion for the armed forces, and, as a career as an officer hadn't been possible, he did the next best thing and taught military education. This meant going from school to school and teaching twelve- to fourteen-year-olds that their homeland had to be defended with weapons. In the lessons at least, he was vastly superior to my father in that he wore a proper uniform.

My father picked up the pace for the last hundred metres. I hated sprint finishes, but I didn't want him to win so I went along with it.

We stood in the hall, panting and sweating. My mother brought us two glasses of Selters water. She was smiling. Herr O had left and the apartment was impeccably tidy. My mother wanted to know about my school day and even asked which route we'd taken for our run. She seemed to be there for us now.

In the middle of the week, a harmonious family afternoon unfolded, steeped in the delicate fug of Duetts and Undine Green Apple.

I woke up in the middle of the night. Someone was ringing from the entrance downstairs. I ran into the hall. My father stood in his pyjamas by the open door, and we waited. I remembered my mother had been out holding a teachers' meeting in the evening. She'd been tetchy and unapproachable for days.

'Where's Mum?' I asked.

'She's just coming,' my father said.

I could hear some shuffling and scuffling. She was having some trouble getting up the stairs.

The first thing I saw was Herr O's head. He was looking round the corner from the landing. His light hair was unkempt and a strand of it hung across his forehead. It took him some effort to bring my mother into view, grasping her tightly around the waist. My mother was clinging to Herr O's neck with one arm and holding a large potted plant in the other. It was a palm.

'Shit, Eckart,' she said.

'We jumped off the flat roof,' Herr O said.

There was a split in my mother's left trouser leg with blood seeping from it. She'd injured her thigh. My father went up to them, took the plant pot from my mother and supported her from the other side. The men hauled her through the front door, which I was holding open. My father had a big grin on his face, which was completely incomprehensible to me in these circumstances. My mother was moaning and swearing. Her blue eyeshadow had spread high up into her eyebrows. Her black mascara had been washed down her cheeks by tears. She hobbled into the living room and flopped down onto the carpet with a loud sigh. Herr O stood in the corridor. He had beads of sweat on his nose.

'Do you need me?' he asked.

My father shook his head. Herr O left, a guilty smile on his lips. I closed the door. My mother had started giggling in the living room.

'Günther gave me a plant,' she said.

I didn't hold out any hope for it. My parents had bad luck with plants. My mother let them dry up; my father drowned them.

My mother smelled of cigarettes and schnapps. I pulled her trousers off; my father emerged from the bathroom with antiseptic and a huge plaster.

'Günther's a poor old sod,' my mother said.

She'd just wanted to come home, but a few colleagues had been making a toast with sparkling wine after the meeting, so she couldn't just leave. And then Günther had suddenly conjured up a bottle of vodka and started on about his broken marriage. My mother spoke in a slurred voice, with tears in her eyes. She seemed so small and limp while she let my father silently treat her wound. She said he'd been sobbing in her arms, and she'd had to comfort him. I didn't know whether to laugh or cry.

My father pressed the plaster onto my mother's thigh. She yelped.

'And how did that happen?' I asked.

They'd been dancing, then they'd climbed through the window onto the flat roof over the main school entrance. Günther had said he'd catch her.

'But he didn't,' my mother said.

She rubbed her smeary eyes. Her leg got caught on that bloody fence, she whimpered.

I imagined drunken teachers jumping from the flat roof of my own school at night-time. I'd never have thought they'd do something like that.

My mother babbled on while my father took her to the bedroom, something about shame and about never being able to go back there again. My father wasn't grinning any more. He wasn't saying anything. It was impossible to work out what he was thinking. Wasn't he angry with my mother? He hated it when she smoked. Or maybe he wanted to calm her down, or comfort her? But who actually had to comfort whom, and why?

My father carried my mother to bed. She was already asleep. I stood in the doorway.

'Go back to bed,' my father said.

I understood. Now was not the time to ask questions.

When I got home, there was a smell of cigarette smoke. But the Undine scent was missing. My father was on a business trip somewhere, with someone, for something important. The brown curtain was drawn. Roger Whittaker was singing. I went into the living room in my socks.

My mother was barefoot, sitting cross-legged on the pale carpet, and Herr O sat with his legs off to one side. A little paunch stuck out over his waistband. The carpet was strewn with sheets of paper covered in writing, photos and envelopes. My mother and Herr O were surrounded by hundreds of letters.

I stepped closer. My mother, her cheeks red and glowing, put her wine glass down on the floor.

'We're looking for a new wife for Günther,' she said.

Herr O looked up at me amicably through his glasses.

'Your mum's being really helpful,' he said.

I said nothing because I couldn't think what to say. There were women in the photos: smiling women with make-up and neat hairdos. Some of them were standing in meadows, some had children in their arms, some wore glasses.

'We have to go about this systematically,' my mother said.

I realized I was disturbing them. I went to my room and sat down on the bed. I'd heard of people advertising like this: I'd read some of the adverts in the magazines and tried to imagine what could be hidden behind so many mysterious abbreviations. I'd wondered what kind of person might need to place a personal advert. Now I knew one. But the fact that this person was sitting with my mother among heaps of women's photos and letters bothered me. What was someone like that doing at ours? And how on earth was my mother going to find the right wife for Herr O in this jumble of papers?

I crept into the corridor and listened. My mother was giggling. Herr O was laughing with his deep voice.

'I can't go for someone who sells shoes for a living,' Herr O was saying.

'You're just being picky,' my mother said.

I pressed myself against the wall and carefully slid one side of my face past the door frame. They didn't notice me. With one eye, I could see my mother sorting the letters into different piles. Herr O had stretched out on the floor and was lighting a cigarette. He was watching my mother with amusement.

Now I understood. My mother could sort all the letters in the world, but Herr O wouldn't find a new wife. He wouldn't find one because the only woman he loved was my mother. But my mother hadn't responded to Herr O's advert because she was happily married to my father. She could let Herr O dote on her, let him entice her into drinking, let him give her houseplants, but she would never exchange my father for him, because Herr O was a reserve lieutenant, a poor old sod and a smoker. And what's more,

I'd recently found out from my mother that Herr O was severely disabled. He'd invited her to the opera on the spur of the moment, but the performance was sold out and there was a long queue at the box office; without a second thought, Herr O walked past the people waiting and up to the window, limping badly as he went. 'Two severely disabled,' he said, and was given two tickets, no questions asked. My mother told me about it at breakfast the next morning after my father had left for work. She sounded emotional and proud as she spoke, and then she lit a Duett.

I crept back to my room. My mother, it was clear, wasn't going to take on a severely disabled reserve old sod. Nevertheless, I tried to imagine what Herr O might be like as a father. I would have enjoyed his deep, calm voice, at least, which held the promise of something like a sense of security.

The time had come. I had begun another school year and I'd graduated from Duetts to Clubs. My heart began to pound when Herr O came into the classroom. He looked smart in his uniform. He placed his briefcase on the teacher's desk and looked at the class. When our eyes met, he grinned at me briefly, just as he and my father had grinned at each other back then. I blushed, but no one noticed.

Herr O talked about NATO and the Warsaw Pact. There were two stars on his epaulettes. My father had just been promoted and now had two stars as well, but his epaulettes had braids too: he was even higher up. Herr O said that all peace-loving forces must be united in defending the achievements of socialism. His voice sounded warm and peace-loving. The others weren't listening to him at all.

Herr O turned on the slide projector. He went from window to window, drawing the heavy curtains. He said he was going to show us the atrocities the imperialist aggressor was capable of. Some of the others started playing battleships. The teacher couldn't see them in the darkened room. Admittedly, what Herr O had to tell us wasn't exactly news, but couldn't they hear him saying it? What a voice!

There was a mushroom cloud on the first slide. I looked at the picture intently to make up for the others' disinterest. The second slide showed children with deformities. I felt sorry for Herr O: surely he could feel how little impact he was having on the others? I concentrated on the mutilated monsters. My belly felt queasy. A tingling sensation started spreading through me. The third slide showed a man with his body covered in blisters. Herr O was saying something about human dignity. My pulse quickened. The man's face was distorted with pain. I began to shiver and my breath was shallow. Raw flesh hung from his bones. The tingling sensation crept up my lower back and engulfed my whole body. I broke out in a cold sweat. The blood-red man became a blur. Herr O's calm voice faded into the distance. Everything went black; I could no longer hear anything. I slid into an abyss.

When I woke up, it was bright and cold. I looked up towards the sky. The heavy curtains were pulled back and the windows were wide open. I was lying on the floor; the others' faces were hovering over me. As white as a sheet, someone said. Herr O's face came closer. Beads of sweat were glistening on his nose. He spoke to me with big, kindly eyes and a voice bathed in concern. It was exactly how he must have bent over my mother after she'd jumped off the flat roof. My mother and I both the worse for wear, lying beneath Herr O, and him looking down on us as if to say it was all his fault.

I wanted to get up. Herr O helped me. He held on to my elbow and my hip. He took me to the staff room and gently sat me down on the sofa.

'I'll call your mum,' he said.

*

My mother changed schools and worked as a headteacher for four years before she was laid off. If the army hadn't been disbanded, my father would have made it to the rank of major general. I started college and visited my parents every two or three weeks.

My father was sitting in the lounge area reading the paper. I was opposite my mother at the dining table. She'd put her feet up.

'Herr O's died,' she said.

'What from?' I said.

'Thrombosis, vascular occlusion.'

My father folded his paper and stood up. I went over to the wall unit and looked for the Roger Whittaker record. I found it. I could almost smell the Duetts and Undine Green Apple. I didn't dare put the record on.

My father came in with the watering can. It was shiny. He'd got into the habit of rubbing it with vinegar solution every week so the limescale wouldn't build up. He walked slowly alongside the window and poured a thin stream of water into the planters. The plants were doing badly, as always. All that water was finishing them off. The roots were rotting and a sallow green colour, and light yellow leaves hung limply over the edges of the pots – no amount of watering can polishing would help. Herr O's palm, however, was flourishing magnificently. My father had repotted it and moved it from the windowsill to the floor because it had grown so large. But that wasn't all. Its leaves had shot up, lush, deep green and perfectly healthy, until they hit the living room ceiling again. My father had constructed a series of hooks and strings up there, which couldn't stop the palm tree's growth, but could at least guide it a little.

My mother brought dinner in from the kitchen. It was potatoes fried with bacon, and eggs. We sat down at the dining table, under a canopy of palm leaves. My father opened a bottle of beer.

'Are you going to the funeral?' I asked.

'No,' my mother said.

THE LETTER

After setting us some classwork, the physics teacher, Herr Schellhorn, crossed his arms on the desk and rested his head on them. He'd been doing that more often lately; the others always giggled, but I was convinced he wasn't well. When upright, his hollow-cheeked head swayed on his wrinkled neck, protruding from his jacket made of Dederon; his skin was grey, his teeth yellow, his lips pale, and his eyes were sunk deep in their sockets and looked like they could have belonged to a pigeon. But Herr Schellhorn was managing less and less to keep his head upright.

I had long since stopped trying to grasp the laws of physics, and while the others were chewing the ends of their pens and poring over the blackboard, I'd keep an eye on the teacher. The index and middle fingers of his left hand, resting on his right elbow, were discoloured yellow, brownish, almost orange – no, now I remember the name of the colour I first heard about in art class: my physics teacher's fingers were ochre, right down to his nails. Herr Schellhorn was bound to have lung cancer.

When I bumped into him in the school corridors and said 'Hello', he'd nod back absent-mindedly; he seemed to prefer passing by unnoticed, without small talk. He was the school's Party Secretary, but I never once heard him say anything political. In fact, he didn't speak much in general, and when he did, he spoke quietly, and only about physics. I wondered how he could be a Party Secretary like that. He would have to debate, gesticulate and agitate for action. But Herr Schellhorn only rested his head in silence. Maybe meetings behind the staffroom door were much more heated. Maybe Herr Schellhorn was more active out of our sight. Maybe he'd jump up from his chair, speak with gusto and win over everyone's hearts with a fiery speech.

The physics room door opened without a knock. A precautionary 'Herr Schellhorn, head up!' almost escaped my lips, but our deputy headmaster and civics teacher, Herr Romberg, had already seen me.

'Tanja! Come with me!'

I was startled and my face went red. Whenever anyone called me by my name, I felt guilty and started blushing. The others giggled. I looked Herr Schellhorn in the eye as I went to the door, sweating and with a hollow feeling in my belly.

In the hallway, Herr Romberg didn't take the usual chummy tone he used to show he was on my side, or more precisely, on my parents' side. This time he acted as if I didn't exist, only grunting as I struggled to keep up with him; his breathing had never seemed so loud. As well as having a nose that was too dry, Herr Romberg was short of spit, and a white secretion would accumulate at the corners of his mouth during the day. If we had civics for our first lesson, it was still bearable, but by midday there were threads of the secretion stretching between his upper and lower lips. It was even worse in the afternoons during our working group sessions on the resistance fighter Anton Saefkow, which only took place every other Wednesday, thank God. By then the secretion had gone from a liquid to a solid state. Herr Romberg drank too little and talked too much. But now he was saying nothing.

'What's this about?' I asked into the silence. My voice was trembling. Herr Romberg said I'd find out in a minute, and fell silent again.

Frau Griebsch sat behind the desk in the middle of the room. She was fat, wore horn-rimmed glasses and never laughed. We respected our headteacher. Herr Romberg sat down on a threadbare chair by the wall. Was that where he normally sat? I stayed where I was. The corner with the artificial leather armchairs was obviously not meant for me.

'Do your parents know about the letter?' Frau Griebsch asked.

She took a typewritten page out of her drawer and held it in front of my face. It was a carbon copy of my letter, just as I'd written it the night before. I'd sent the original to the Ministry of National Education and I'd given my first carbon copy to Frau Gawiol that morning. But how had Frau Griebsch got hold of my letter?

'Do your parents know about this letter?'

'Yes.'

I searched for her eyes behind her horn-rimmed glasses.

'And? What do they think about it?'

'They think it's good.'

'I see. And you've already sent it off. To the Ministry.'

I nodded.

Frau Griebsch looked at Herr Romberg. He lowered his gaze and grunted.

'But my father reworked the letter with me first.'

That was a lie, but I didn't feel up to the situation on my own. Frau Griebsch must have got the wrong end of the stick. Only my father could save me now.

'Well,' said Frau Griebsch, and suddenly I saw her tiny eyes flashing. She didn't start shouting; she squeezed the words out from between her clenched teeth.

'Next time, maybe you could let us know beforehand.'

'Will do,' I said, biting my tongue. I'd meant to show I understood but had accidentally sounded like I was being cheeky again. Frau Griebsch showed me the door. There would be no next time: that much had become clear to me right away.

I slowly started down the corridor, but Herr Romberg grabbed me by the shoulder and turned me to face him. I was precisely the last person he would have expected such deceitful behaviour from, he said, I must immediately retract the letter and apologize to the Ministry, Frau Griebsch, my parents and, above all, him. That letter was a vile slander and a breach of trust. He was disappointed in me, and he now knew where he stood in the future.

I sat down halfway up the stairs. I could feel how hot my face was when I put my head in my ice-cold hands. I felt sick. Why had she done that? Why had Frau Gawiol passed the letter on to the headteacher, quick as a wink, as they say? I'd been thinking about her all the time while I was writing it. After all, she was the one whose cheeks would go red as she told us exciting stories that weren't in the schoolbooks: like the one about the trucks the Party used to send to the countryside to play Russian marching music to the farmers until they agreed to join the Agricultural Production Cooperative, worn down but united. I'd written the letter because I wanted to be like Frau Gawiol. I'd given her, and her alone, the letter that morning because I wanted her to like me. And yes, I'd even dared to hope she'd give me some praise.

The bell rang. My things were still in the physics room. I ran upstairs and caught up with the others who were going up another flight of stairs for the rest of that Monday: two hours of Russian, then home.

At the dinner table, I told my parents about being summoned to the office. I heard my mother fling her fork down on her plate before I looked up from mine. She'd stopped eating, and with her cheeks half-full, she was glaring reproachfully at me and my father, who was still chewing peacefully. Then she erupted. Why did I have to write letters like that, instead of going to our country cabin with her at the weekend? I had plenty of better things to do: I should be learning my physics or clearing out the shitty rabbit hutch. It was most embarrassing for her – my teachers all knew she was headteacher at a nearby school. The Ministry would definitely want to talk to her. And all this with the next Pedagogical Council just around the corner! And anyway, she couldn't stand that Romberg, the bootlicker!

My father kept eating and remained silent. My mother couldn't sit still. She stood up. She started lashing out at him from above, pointing her finger at him.

'You let her stay at home, didn't you! You read that letter! You were going to change it! But you don't care – you're above it all. Take that grin off your face, Comrade Colonel!'

She ran to her bedroom. The door slammed, and we heard the key turning in its lock. She was obviously crying.

It was true: my father did have a grin on his face, and he was grinning at me now, too. But that was all. Why wasn't he doing anything? Why wasn't he helping me? Where was the quiet 'I'll sort it out' to save me, to take the burden off my shoulders: without his backing, I'd never have sent the letter. Why didn't he reach for his address book and call any of the numbers next to his code names? Why was he just sitting there grinning? He'd never let me down like this before. At least he wasn't shouting, though I had no idea why. And as forlorn as I felt, I clung to this.

'We should've taken out the more forthright bits,' my father said.

He served himself another helping of fried potatoes and poured the last of the beer into his glass.

The night before, after he'd read the letter, he'd nodded appreciatively and suggested that it should be left as it was – 'Just take out a few of the more forthright bits,' he'd added.

I hadn't wanted to. My letter was good, and Frau Gawiol would like it, I was sure of that. Also, if we'd taken out the more forthright bits, I'd have had to type the whole thing out again. So I'd pulled the original version out of my father's grasp, put it in the envelope, addressed it to the Ministry of National Education and done up my boots. I'd felt proud of myself and my father, and I knew my father was proud of himself, and of me too. On the way back from the postbox, I'd lit a Sieger cigarette.

Now we were clearing the dinner table in silence.

'Just wait and see,' my father said, opening his newspaper. My mother would calm down and come out of the bedroom soon.

I went to my room. If I'd known what I'd be setting off with those typed pages, I'd have happily taken out all the forthright bits I could find, right up until the sheets of paper were completely white and blank in front of me once more.

I decided to excuse myself from school the next day with period pains; PE with Frau Gawiol was the first lesson, so it sounded believable. Although it was only half past seven, I switched off the light, wrapped a scarf around my neck and pulled the covers over my head.

Three days later, during the morning break, I heard a shrill whistle, followed by a screech: 'Tanja!'

I blushed, turned round and saw Frau Gawiol in the corridor in the distance, beckoning me over. I pushed my way through the other students to reach her. She was wearing a tracksuit and plimsolls. A metal whistle hung from her neck and she was holding a few files and a history book. With her red cheeks, Frau Gawiol always looked so healthy. When I stood in front of her, I noticed for the first time that I was quite a bit taller than her. Frau Gawiol spoke very quietly.

'Listen here, how dare you take the things I tell you in class and write to the Ministry about them? And completely out of context! Who do you think you are? I've never seen anything as sly, in all my twenty years as a teacher! That's the last straw, my girl, the last straw!'

'I didn't mean it like that.'

'Didn't mean it like that? History has a word for what you've done, my girl, and that word is betrayal!'

Frau Gawiol's words came hissing out of her, and it was as if she were burrowing into me from below, her back hunched over and her head twisted upwards. We'd never been so close to one another before, and although tears were obscuring my vision, I could suddenly see that the red cheeks I liked so much weren't red cheeks at all: there were hundreds of dark red broken veins across them, as if her face had a net laid over both sides. Frenzied scribbles covered Frau Gawiol's face. It was a sophisticated kind of war paint that would deceive and attract the enemy from a distance with its bright red, only to instil fear at close range.

While Frau Gawiol was hissing and I was sobbing, an ambulance siren became gradually louder. Two paramedics ran up the steps with a stretcher and came back down: on the stretcher was Herr Schellhorn, his face white as chalk and his eyes closed. A few curious students lined their path. The paramedics left the school building through the main entrance, Herr Schellhorn between them. Was he going to die?

Frau Gawiol started again.

'Frau Griebsch asked me to inform you that a representative from the Ministry will be visiting the school. He will be talking to you, with the headteacher in attendance. Wednesday, three o'clock sharp in the headteacher's office. And I'd advise you to keep your mouth shut if you don't want to make things any worse! Is that clear?'

'Yes.'

'And now off with you!'

Frau Gawiol stalked away. I went back outside.

'And Tanja! Wear your Free German Youth shirt!'

I turned round and nodded vehemently enough for her to see it from a distance.

People must have been on the phone to each other. It must have been Frau Griebsch to my father, my father to the Ministry and the Ministry to Frau Griebsch. Or maybe not. Who knows? In any case, no one had replied to my letter yet. But now there was this visit.

The night before that Wednesday, I couldn't get to sleep. It was just before midnight. I lay in bed and read the letter for the hundredth time. The second carbon copy I'd kept was barely legible: the letters were like shadows, the full stops holes. By now I knew the letter off by heart, word for word, sentence for sentence, but the more I read it, the more alien it became to me. It was as if someone else had written it.

I usually slept with my physics file under my pillow, in the hope that the facts would slip into my brain. But that night I put the letter there instead. Then I wrapped my scarf around my neck, turned off the light and pulled the covers over my head.

I couldn't say what moved me about it. It was nothing more than an image, but it had stayed with me ever since I first came across it in a play: hundreds of soldiers racing across the battlefield, screaming for their mothers, the front behind them, and their homeland ahead. From that image, the story started to flow – it started to move and took me along with it. My fear spread to the soldiers around me, and we began to walk, over dead bodies, over barren land, across meadows, through fields, past figures on pedestals, past display cabinets with open books and staged photos of victors, past a hero in a glass coffin; then we started to run; we were running alongside a train bringing my grandma from Breslau; she had two suitcases and four children with her, three beside her and one in her belly – that was my mother; my mother was playing on the bunker in the cornfield next to the tracks; my grandpa was returning home from the War with prison clothes and a wooden leg; he took my mother, so sickly, so weak, onto his lap: 'You're a warchild, the

Soviets give you sugar cubes and smile at you; just eat, my child, we'll breed pigeons, it's all right, it's all right.'

Had I had any sleep at all? I tucked my Free German Youth shirt into my bag, next to my files, taking care not to crumple it.

Seven school hours passed by. At ten minutes to three, I knocked on the secretary's office door. I knocked a second time, a little harder. Herr Romberg opened the door. The white secretion in the corners of his mouth had already turned to paste. He led me to the headteacher's office. I went in and saw that the corner with the armchairs was full of people. On the table were half-empty coffee cups, Selters glasses, biscuits; things had been jolly, I could tell, but now their expressions were serious.

The blood rushed to my head and began to thunder in my ears. Frau Griebsch stood up from her chair and introduced me to the man from the Ministry. He stood up too. I couldn't hear his name over the thundering in my head. I gave him my hand. It was damp.

'Good afternoon.'

I wasn't sure if the man had understood me: I could feel an enormous pressure in my ears, just like the summer before when we'd flown to the Black Sea, and my voice was echoing inside me as if my head was going round in space, in an invisible capsule.

'Thank you for your letter. I read it – it was very interesting,' the man from the Ministry said, if my thundering didn't deceive me, and then he sat down again.

'All in all, Tanja's a very good student,' said Frau Griebsch. The man and Frau Griebsch smiled, and I dared to take a closer look at the sofa. There sat Frau Gawiol, with her red cheeks, and Herr Romberg, who was smiling encouragingly at me, and jammed in their midst, his arms crossed and his head bowed, was Herr Schellhorn in a dove-blue lab coat. I would have liked to give him a smile, but Herr Schellhorn wasn't looking at me: he was pale and silent, his eyes half-closed, like a corpse. At that moment, we all realized I was still standing while everyone else was seated and there was nowhere else to sit. At a tiny nod from Frau Griebsch, Herr Romberg jumped up, fetched his threadbare chair and pushed it into the back of my knees.

'Thank you.'

I sat down. It was echoey in my capsule. I could hear scraps of conversation, such as 'engagement is welcome', 'guiding students properly', 'questions are allowed', 'not raising a generation of cowards', 'getting the tone right sometimes', 'always ready to listen', 'clearing up potential misunderstandings'.

No grim looks; no reproachful grunts. And no one insisted on the official apology I'd prepared the night before, all alone under the covers, without my father's help.

While the adults were talking, I was making the nicest possible face with just a hint of hangdog eyes. And then a strange thought struck me: why had Frau Gawiol kept on talking when Herr Schellhorn was being carried out of the school, without so much as a word about it? And why hadn't Herr Romberg done anything when he came to get me from the physics room? He must have seen Herr Schellhorn collapsed in his chair, his arms flopped out on the teacher's desk and his head resting on them. Was I the only one for miles around who was worried about him? And why weren't they doing anything now, as Herr Schellhorn sat between them, pale and motionless on the sofa? It was as if they hadn't even noticed him. Day after day, they dragged this dying shadow of a man along with them, ignoring him with all their might.

The man from the Ministry stood up, Frau Griebsch followed suit, and then everyone else. They shook hands and wished each other well. Frau Griebsch and Herr Romberg walked us to the door like a married couple would with old friends. It hadn't even been fifteen minutes. Frau Gawiol dashed off, Herr Schellhorn crept away and suddenly I was alone with the man from the Ministry. He led me to the main entrance and held the door open for both of us.

'Well? How did you find our discussion?'

'Short.'

The man laughed.

'Your letter did the rounds in our department as soon as we got it. We've never had a student reacting to our books before. They only ever write in during educational conferences.'

We'd stopped in front of the school entrance. It was good to get some fresh air; my thundering was gradually subsiding.

'To be honest,' I said, 'at school I just got into trouble about it.'

The man put down his briefcase and buttoned his coat.

'Everyone needs to protect themselves,' he said. I nodded, although I didn't really know what he meant. He had a warm voice.

And then I started talking. I talked about Frau Gawiol's funny stories, which were much more interesting than what was in the curriculum, and about the theatre, which was much more exciting than lessons, and even about trousers in the West, which looked a thousand times better than ours, and as I spoke, my teeth were chattering because I only had my blue shirt on under my anorak, but I talked and talked and only went quiet when it got dark all of a sudden and we could see inside the one room in the school with the light still on; in the small, illuminated square, we could see Frau Griebsch sitting at her desk and Herr Romberg taking two brandy glasses and a bottle out of the cupboard. It was like a shadow play at the fair. He poured out a glass and handed it to her. They threw their heads back and drank.

The man from the Ministry gave my hand a firm squeeze and said I was welcome to write to him again; after all, I'd still be at school for a few more years.

'Yes, well, we'll see,' I said. Then I ran off, shivering but happy.

RUCKEDIGU

The hallway, with its walls covered with framed certificates, was so narrow that only one person could get ready in it at a time. I looked through the crack in the kitchen doorway; I could see all the coats hanging up, and my grandpa Walter squeezed between them, sitting on the stool, lacing up his boots. They were the only ones my grandpa owned: custom-made boots with endlessly long laces. He started with the left one, on his wooden leg. He hooked up the laces one at a time, pulling them taut. When he reached the top of his wooden calf, he made a tight double bow and let his thick, faded corduroy trouser leg fall over the brown imitation leather. Then he spotted me: 'Ruckedigu,' he said, and I laughed.

He took less time on his right foot. He gathered his strength then stood up; he buttoned his jacket up to his pale, wrinkly neck and straightened his flat cap on his bald head in the wardrobe mirror. He went out into the yard towards the garage and I heard the front door closing behind him, slow and heavy. Now it was my turn: I slipped on my boots and anorak, wrapped myself in my scarf and tied my white fur hat under my chin. I tugged at the iron doorknob and went outside and waited. The air was cold and had a burnt smell about it. I could see my breath. The scrap metal wagons were squealing on the tracks that ran past the house, as they slowly made their way to the steelworks. At the end of the last wagon, two men in orange helmets, vests and gloves were standing on the steps, gripping rusty poles. One of them cheerfully raised a hand to greet us. His face was smeared with soot. My grandpa waved back. He was halfway to the garage. I ran past him and waited at the door, which was covered with dark grey roofing felt.

The garage was really a shed: a low wooden structure which fit snugly around the 'vehicle'. My grandpa opened the padlock, pushed the two doors wide open – jamming wedges under them with his wooden foot – and squeezed past the vehicle into the darkness. I stood two or three metres away and watched him manoeuvre the vehicle backwards out of the garage. He clutched the windscreen surround with his left hand, and with his right he reached through the unfastened transparent cover into the vehicle's interior, to the handlebars, and pulled with all his might. In this crooked stance, he had to drag his wooden leg. Once he got it moving, he carefully rolled the vehicle out into the open, and then, shifting his weight in the opposite direction to brake, he brought the vehicle to a stop.

My grandpa Walter always called it 'the vehicle' because it was neither a car nor a motorbike: it looked like a cube on three wheels. My grandpa had had it sprayed a blueish-grey shade and he'd spent days fitting a Trabant roof onto it. Where once a wayward plastic canopy had stretched, ingrained with soot, a freshly polished top now perched, with rounded, chrome-plated edges, which glinted from afar.

I imagined the vehicle as a performing bear cub: the three narrow wheels which had to carry its chunky body seemed like crooked little legs to me; the flapping side covers, which would catch the wind, were an ill-fitting dancer's dress; and someone had put a crown on the bear cub's head which was much too large for it, so it couldn't see properly. By cherishing and nurturing it, my grandpa had won its trust and the bear cub faithfully carried out his every wish to the best of its ability.

My grandpa bent over to reach the starter at the vehicle's side. He tugged on it as hard as he could. The vehicle rattled, jerked and fell silent again. If the nights were cold, it would always take him a few tries to get it started. But they dug deep, my grandpa and the vehicle, and at the fourth go the engine fired up. My grandpa wrenched open the driver's door and took his seat behind the handlebars. He grabbed his wooden leg with both hands and let it drop into the footwell. Then he slammed the door shut and turned the throttle knob with his right hand. The vehicle let out a squeal.

My grandma Hildegard came out of the front door. She'd only make an appearance when she could hear he'd got the vehicle started. Her freshly combed white forelocks peeked out from under her knitted hat. The ends of her shawl lay flat on top of each other, pressed onto her chest by the collar of her quilted coat. My grandma rattled the house keys. She locked up as if she was going to Australia for three months, and then slipped the bunch of keys into her handbag, zipping it shut. She had a shopping bag full of empty milk bottles in her right hand, and her handbag and the tatty footstool in her left. My grandma took short, quick steps to the vehicle where my grandpa was waiting. He leaned to the right, took the bag of bottles from her and pushed it under the seats. My grandma got in. She tucked her handbag in front of her belly and placed the footstool between her legs. Now it was my turn: I manoeuvred my bottom onto the footstool, drew in my legs and carefully turned to face forward, wrapping my arms around my knees. My grandma tucked me in a little and slammed the door. She rattled the aluminium handle to make sure it was closed. We were in – all three of us. We were ready to go.

'Off to town!' my grandpa cried out. We were going to the Gröditz branch of Konsum for our shopping.

I was sitting low down in the vehicle; my grandma had stowed me away so well that I couldn't see out of the window, yet I knew exactly where we were. I recognized the journey from the three turnings my grandpa had to steer the vehicle through. Braking was essential before the first corner: I felt him give way before going left out of the yard into the main street. The vehicle began to wobble and gently shake us, so our winter coats rustled against each other: a second, unmistakable sign that we'd reached the cobbled road. Then I heard a bright, steady beep – the same one that stole through my grandparents' windows even at night, accompanied by red hazard lights shining into the dark rooms. My grandpa braked again. The steelworks railway barrier lowered, as it always seemed to whenever we went shopping.

'We're first in the queue,' my grandma said. I could hear the squeal of the scrap metal wagons and saw my grandpa raising two fingers to his flat cap in greeting. 'There goes Heinz Finkel. He must be on earlies this week,' he said.

If I kept my head straight, my gaze fell directly on the empty glove compartment. If I turned round, my grandma would nervously pat my hat, flattening it and pushing me down. She was afraid that someone would look into the vehicle and spot me. Strictly speaking, she was right to worry: the vehicle was called the Krause Duo, and that meant that an inventor named Krause had designed it to transport just two people. It had been issued to my grandpa and he'd needed a disability note to get it. Even his upgrades to the roof and paintwork had inscribed worry lines onto my grandma's face. My grandpa said my grandma Hildegard was driving him crazy with her fussing. I threw my head back until it landed in my grandma's lap and sent peals of laughter up from below. Her handbag handles fell into my face, and my forehead brushed against her bosom – which was contained by a huge bra with cups that I could fit over my head – and I laughed even louder. My grandpa winked at me. I could see the hair growing out of his nostrils and the sharp point of his Adam's apple under the sagging skin of his neck. The barrier rose up, and my grandpa turned his smiling eyes to the cobblestones and accelerated. We took the long bend around the steelworks; now I could see the grey sky, the chimneys and the top of the dirty concrete wall which enclosed the steelworks like a thick, heavy belt. We passed the clubhouse and crossed the bridge over the Röder. The Krause Duo rattled, puffed and bumped along through Gröditz, while I laughed, jammed between my grandma's thighs.

Ten to fifteen young men were squatting, lying and lounging together on a single metal-framed bed. They were wearing washed-out striped pyjamas, and they had caps on their shaved skulls. The men had pale, thin faces, but their eyes shone. They were laughing at the camera as if they were having a blast. My grandma was reluctant to get out the photo; I often begged to see it, but most of the time she wouldn't give in. Sometimes she'd get angry and say the weather had been better before the War, that the planes were to blame for it, that they'd made a racket like thunder and lightning. She'd complain that none of this or that would have happened in the past.

If I managed to persuade my grandma, she'd dig the photo out of the tin she kept hidden in the deepest corner of the living room dresser. We'd sit next to each other on the sofa; she would finger the photo from every side or stroke it with the palm of her hand. The thick paper would bend; the edges were rough. It might once have been black and white, but now it was light and dark grey with a tinge of yellow. With her reading glasses on, she'd hold it close to her face and point to a thin man with a long, narrow nose who was sitting at the very front of the bed grinning at us.

'There's Grandpa in the Lazarett,' she'd say, with plenty

of compassion and a hint of pride. I'd never heard the word 'Lazarett' before, and I didn't know anyone else who used it. She seemed to like it, as she said it more often than necessary. The word sounded beautiful.

I suspected that 'Lazarett' was an old word for a holiday camp and that the men looked so haggard because they were leaving the next day and had been up all night: they'd dressed up as zebras for the farewell party and had snapped one last group photo before they stripped their beds, tidied their rooms and got on the bus which would take them home.

When I found out that the 'Lazarett' was a hospital for wounded soldiers and that my grandpa had been in the War for six years, I finally understood how he'd got his wooden leg. I'd heard about shrapnel ripping off men's arms and legs, but my grandma never spoke about it. Instead, she'd say that every time he'd been on leave from the front, Walter had left her a little something to keep her busy. Then she'd lean in close, wink at me with a smirk and touch her breasts with her soft, veiny hands. They'd grown so big; how good it was that she'd had so much milk.

My grandpa manoeuvred the vehicle into the garage and locked up. My grandma went back to the house to put away the shopping, and we made our way to the allotment: my grandpa and I walking side by side, his wooden leg making more of a crunch in the sand, and me twisting the balls of my feet into the ground as I walked to make deeper footprints. Paint was peeling from the allotment fences, revealing previous layers of colour. In the summer, the weight of the brambles would warp the rotten fence slats. My grandma had forbidden me from eating the berries unwashed: the black wasn't a sign they were ripe, she'd told me, raising her eyebrows conspiratorially, it was actually soot. I reached for my grandpa's dry, bony hand.

'Are you going to feed them now?' I asked.

'They have to go for a fly first.'

My grandma had her vegetable patch in the front section of the allotment. The area further back belonged to Grandpa Walter and the pigeons. Over the years, he'd cobbled together a fortress for himself and his pigeons. Feed sacks, scraps of wood and rusty tools were stored under lean-tos of various heights, sections built on top of each other, repaired several times with pieces of grey roofing felt. I wound my way past bulky wire mesh and damp walls to the pigeon loft, which was the heart of Walter's wooden cave and towered over it by a good two metres. The pigeon loft looked like the picture of the witch Baba Yaga's house in one of my fairy tale books. Her house was up in the air, supported by a chicken's foot which clawed into the earth, all bones and cartilage, huge and wrinkled. I'd often open my book at that page and wonder where the rest of the monstrous hen had gone.

My grandpa climbed the steep wooden stairs on the rear wall, taking them one step at a time, planting his right foot and pulling the wooden one after it. There was no banister. I could see why my grandma hadn't graced Walter's kingdom with her presence for years; she would have been scared to death. My grandpa opened the latch, pushed open the squeaky door and ducked under the door frame. Now it was my turn. As I climbed the stairs on all fours, I could already hear them cooing, loud and incessant: 'ruckedigu, ruckedigu'. I stepped carefully onto the wooden floor, which was covered with chalk-white spots. I left the door ajar and stood in the corner. When it came out fresh and thick from under their tails, pigeon poo wasn't just white – it had grey and black bits in it so it looked a mottled grey. I'd often noticed that at Schönhauser Allee S-Bahn station or at the Alexanderplatz fountain. But as soon as it dried, just the white remained and it ate into any surface, even stone. The floorboards in the pigeon loft were almost whitewashed with all the layers of it. It didn't smell bad: it was a dusty smell, like dry grain.

The pigeons had long since raised the alarm, and every last one flapped out of their nest boxes, each of which had a little swinging door. My grandpa had put fifty or sixty of these boxes on the right-hand wall; it looked like the pigeons slept in an enormous advent calendar. They ran frantically around my grandpa's feet, their heads jerking tirelessly and their neck plumage shimmering from silvery into green, pink and violet. They strutted over the wood on their scrawny legs like wind-up toy soldiers; they skittered about on clawed feet the colour of bruises. Whenever their paths crossed, they'd seamlessly take a new route to avoid each other, crowding into a space of five or six square metres, with zigzagging paths which had no end and only one goal: Walter. They sought him out, outdoing one another with their cooing for him, closing and opening their bald, crisp-edged eyelids, as if they were frantic to photograph everything in front of their lens, everything, and most of all him, from a thousand perspectives. My grandpa's appearance had triggered a frenzied attack of how-do-you-do's and ruckedigu's.

I stood in my corner without moving and watched my grandpa bend down and reach for a pigeon. Its plumage alternated between white and blueish-grey – he called that sort of pigeon a 'grizzle'. He held it very firmly, pressing its wings to its body with both hands, and lifted it up to head height, stretching out his arms to inspect the pigeon from a distance. It stayed very still and let itself be looked at. My grandpa seemed to be checking something. He passed his eyes over it as he gently turned it back and forth in the dim light falling through the streaky, almost opaque windows of the pigeon loft. I would have liked to have Walter's hands at that moment, holding the soft, warm pigeon's body, feeling its plumage, its muscles, its bones. My grandpa mumbled a few words: I couldn't tell whether he was talking to himself or to the pigeon. He released the bird, and with two or three flaps of its wings, it landed in the narrow space amidst its peers, stirring up feathers and dust and causing a new wave of turmoil among the others, obliged to remain on the floor.

My grandpa climbed onto a stool, speckled with pigeon droppings, in front of the windows. When he had to, my grandpa could be really agile. He stretched up to the loft's gable and turned two bent nails to one side, flipping a wooden board – no bigger than the boards my grandma served our bread on in the evenings – away from the wall. Now, the hatch was open. The pigeons understood. There was an enormous stampede. The ones that fluttered up but didn't make it out were forced aside and had to try again. Only two, or at most three, could fit on the board at once. They squeezed through the gap into the open air and flew off.

I'd managed to persuade my grandma. She turned the photo over and over, stroking it and saying that beautiful word again. I sat next to her, imagining my mother, my two aunts and my uncle suckling on my grandma's breasts. I looked at the young men in stripes in Hildegard's hands. They were laughing, and as I wondered what they had been talking about, I noticed that my grandpa, grinning at the front of the bed, had two legs made of flesh and blood. The shock struck me to my core. They peeked out from the bottom of his pyjama trousers and were tucked into lumpy slippers made of felt. They looked the same as each other, white and thin and real.

'Where's Grandpa's wooden leg?' I interrupted my grandma, who was saying something about air raid warnings and cellars. I'd never seen my grandpa with two legs of his own. She looked at me in astonishment and shook her head. I could see from her face that she thought I was a halfwit who needed to have her times tables drummed into her for the umpteenth time.

'Grandpa lost his leg much later,' she said.

It took me a lot of effort to get the story straight and banish the idea of his leg being blown off. My grandpa had come back from the War with two healthy legs. The shrapnel I'd heard about had injured his neck and back. He'd worked in the steelworks for twenty years, working shifts with the scrap metal until the accident happened, not long before he retired. He used to unload the scrap which arrived at the steelworks on freight trains around the clock. He would climb among the bigger pieces on the wagons and pull them out to be melted down in the blast furnace. One night, for some unknown reason, a piece of scrap exploded and flew up in the air. He had the presence of mind to jump off the wagon, but he landed in the scrap and broke his foot. His ankle was shattered; the fracture was complicated and the bones didn't want to grow back together again. His foot festered and he always had blood in his shoe. Inch by inch the open wound crept up his leg until, after two years, the doctors decided to amputate it. They severed it below the knee. My grandpa got a prosthesis and he learned how to walk again using crutches. But the phantom pain went on and on, his stump was sore and swollen and it chafed all over. They often had to take the ambulance service to Riesa to see the orthopaedist. My grandpa was declared disabled; he had four more years to go until retirement.

'Luckily,' my grandma said, her face assuming an expression of formal gravity, 'the state health insurance provided him with the vehicle. And,' she said proudly, 'the prosthesis is custom-made.'

My grandpa locked the allotment gate and I took his hand. We walked along the sandy path, past the rotten fences. We stopped by the brambles.

They were flying in convoy. Not one went off course. A flock of pigeons, constantly changing its shape, swiftly and smoothly circled above us. Sometimes they swooped down close to the loft, almost brushing it as they passed, as if to make sure their home was still there and would take them back. They soared over the TV antennas on the grimy roofs; they drifted away, flitted over the steelworks chimneys like a shadow, piercing the yellow smoke. Every time they disappeared beyond the horizon, I was scared they wouldn't ever find their way back again, but then they would reappear, albeit not always where I thought they'd be. They steadily rose, fell, floated. And anyone who happened to be looking up at the grey sky in Gröditz – sweaty steelworkers ending their shift, pensioners peeking out from behind their curtains, kindergarten children walking two by two – could see that Walter Stasch had let his pigeons out to paint beautiful, invisible shapes in the air.

'Come on, my little pidge,' my grandpa said, 'Grandma's waiting.'

My grandma's soft, swollen spaghetti was the best in the entire world. I never knew if she accidentally cooked it for too long because she always had to wait for us, or if she did it on purpose to spare her and Walter's false teeth. She sat down with us at the table, and announced that, at the weekend, she'd cook us a pigeon. She looked at my grandpa. His face became serious, almost formal. The grizzle: he said he thought it should be the grizzle.

I wasn't allowed to watch, but I knew how he did it. My grandpa would put the pigeon on the chopping block in the garden and cut off its head and feet with his hatchet. My grandma had told me how it was done, her face apprehensive. The bird would carry on flapping its wings for a long while, blood spurting from its neck, and only when it had lost its fight would my grandpa take the pigeon to the kitchen where my grandma would bleed it out over the sink, pluck it, gut it and cook a soup out of its meat and bones. When she brought the soup to the table, my grandma would fish around in it until she had the firm little pigeon's heart in her spoon, and put it on my plate. I would always save it until the end, and my grandparents would watch reverently as I ate it up.

After lunch, my grandpa pushed his plate aside, crossed his arms on the table and, without so much as a glance in our direction, rested his head on them. He had a habit of taking his afternoon nap while he sat at the table. I'd never have been able to sleep in such an uncomfortable position and I always wondered where he'd learned it. My grandma carefully put the dishes in the enamel washing-up bowl so he wouldn't be woken by any clattering. We crept into the living room. I lay on the sofa so I could look out of the window at the wall of the steelworks. My grandma spread a blanket over me and silently stroked my cheeks, before sitting down in the TV chair with the paper and her reading glasses. I could hear my grandpa in the kitchen, breathing deeply and evenly, and the clock on the dresser ticking. The muffled tones of the barrier's perky jingling rang through the living room. There was a rustle. The paper had slipped out of my grandma's hand onto the floor. Her head stretched far back on the chair's headrest, her mouth was slightly open, a little snore embellishing the silence.

'Grandpa got his first pigeon when he was seven,' my grandma said; 'his mother died so young.' She always said this with a very sad voice, as if it had happened just the day before. And she never mentioned one of these facts without the other. I combined the two as well and imagined that Walter's mother only gave her son a pigeon so she could die, and that the pigeon replaced his mother from then on. I knew from *Grimms' Fairy Tales* that only the pigeons remained faithful to Cinderella after her mother died.

Grandpa had kept pigeons all his life, bar the one interruption – the War. When he was drafted into the army, he had to leave his pigeons behind in Breslau, and that seemed worse than leaving Hildegard behind and getting caught in a hail of shrapnel. My grandma wondered what had become of the pigeons without Walter there for them. The apartment building in Breslau, with the pigeon loft my grandpa had built in the attic, disappeared; they once took the bus back to the city, by then called Wrocław, to look for it, but they couldn't find it. My grandma had had to leave her belongings and her home there overnight; she'd got on an overcrowded train heading west with a big belly, three children and two suitcases. She had nothing but a scrap of paper with the address of her cousin, who lived in Gröditz. She showed the paper to the conductor, and when it was light the next morning, the conductor said, 'This is Elsterwerda, here's where you get off.' He pointed in one direction, his arm outstretched. They walked along paths and bumpy roads; it was a cold February. When the children cried, she gave them sugar water, and she asked people she met on the way for directions. They found her cousin's house, and he took them in and let them stay in the attic. My grandma looked at me with shining eyes, cheerful and God-fearing. The packed trains all went on to Dresden, where they were bombed, along with all the passengers.

'I'm going to the pigeon loft,' my grandpa said. I jumped up from the sofa and scurried past him into the narrow hallway and put on my boots, anorak and hat as fast as I could.

'Don't be late back,' I heard my grandma calling, 'it's bath night.'

We kept an eye out for the pigeons on the way. I spotted them far off, above the steelworks. I thought they'd ventured further than ever before; they'd grown bolder and the circles they made had become larger. My fear of them disappearing, never to be seen again, was something I kept to myself.

The pigeon loft was empty. My grandpa dragged a heavy paper sack out of the corner, took off the clothes pegs keeping it closed and rolled down its stiff top. He used an old, bent soup spoon to shovel grain into the wooden trough running along the floorboards. As he did so, he began to whistle softly. His lips scarcely pursed, he produced a high-pitched tone. It had a tender sound. My grandpa rarely needed to stop whistling to catch his breath. He reached into a tin, threw six handfuls of corn kernels onto the rest of the feed and gave me the soup spoon. 'Mix,' he said, and carried on whistling. I crouched in front of the trough and stirred the corn into the other seeds. The grains were heavy; the spoon had to push against a fair bit of resistance. I used my hands to distribute the feed, smoothing it out with my palms and taking care to make it the same height all the way down the long trough, even at the furthest ends. After that, justice would prevail. My grandpa carried on whistling as the first pigeons flew down to the hatch from different directions. They furiously flapped their wings to brake as they landed on a board outside. They used the tiny walkway to get in and flapped down to the ground, where they dashed to the feeding trough without the slightest zigzag or detour and started eating. Through the windows I could see the pigeons flying towards the hatch; if the board was too crowded and they had no room to land, they'd turn sharply and soar upwards again. They had to circle in a queue over the allotments until it was their turn. The pigeon loft filled up, the pecking and cooing grew louder and my grandpa was still whistling. Walter's tender, constant call had reached even the ones who'd been far off, high up in the sky.

He sat down on the stool and pushed a footstool with peeling white varnish towards me. I sat down on it. My grandpa took a pack of F6 cigarettes and a box of matches out of his jacket pocket. He stopped whistling and lit one. He knocked the ashes into a schnapps glass with a few cigarette butts at the bottom of it. The pigeons were pecking and cooing in the silence. They stood as if they were threaded together before the wooden trough, all in a row, tirelessly poking their beaks into the grain, like a piano keyboard played by an invisible hand. I looked at my grandpa.

'All in,' I said.

'One's still not back,' he replied.

'Grandpa came back home late,' my grandma said, 'but he did come back. One day he was standing in the doorway, so thin, pale and tired. "I'm back," he said. It was spring, and the baby had been around for almost a year.' At first she barely recognized him; his hair had fallen out. He must have seen the horror in her eyes. She gave him something to eat. His uniform was so dirty it could stand up on its own; he'd torn off his epaulettes. He took his mess kit from his belt. She pulled his muddy boots off his feet. He'd come by train, and he'd asked for directions from Elsterwerda. He showed her his discharge letter. He lay down on the bed in the attic and fell asleep.

'For a long time he smelled so strange,' my grandma said, 'of disinfectant.'

He soon began to breed pigeons again, and although in the first few years everything was scarce, he always found food for the birds. My grandpa joined the Association of Small Animal Breeders and was elected to the local Gröditz group's committee. Over the years, he won all those certificates and trophies that were still on display in the apartment. 'Until the accident,' my grandma said, 'pigeon racing was his be all and end all.'

My grandpa spent summer Sundays in his wooden cave, smoking, climbing up and down the ladder, staring nervously up at the sky. Whether Hildegard could fathom it or not, he simply couldn't sit down for lunch, cool as a cucumber, whenever one of his competition pigeons might be about to arrive home. My grandma stopped moaning, put the lunch in his old mess kit and took it to her husband in the loft.

As early as two days before a race, the birds were stowed into baskets and the numbers stamped into the aluminium rings around the pigeons' legs were added to competition lists. The baskets were loaded onto a van, which would make its way to Budapest, Prague or Sofia overnight. My grandma uttered the names of these cities, places she and my grandpa had never been, with a mixture of awe and wanderlust. Among the breeders, they were known as 'liberation sites'. On the Sunday morning at five or six o'clock, once the sun had risen, the pigeons were released. All the baskets would be opened in one swoop. As my grandma spoke, I could hear the thousands of powerful wings flapping and feel the force with which the birds escaped from their dark confinement and blasted up into the sky. They chased up and away in a torrent into the cool, sunny morning air. They flew very quickly and purposefully, covering hundreds of miles with only one thing in mind: home. My grandpa would stand on the wooden steps, smoking with an unsteady hand, searching the sky over and over. The first one would reach home after seven or eight hours. It would touch down in the hatch, its little heart pounding violently in its breast. My grandpa's heart would be beating wildly too, and he'd pick it up, pull the ring from its leg and put it in the special clock that would record its time. He'd stroke the pigeon, talk to it and praise it. Its feed and fresh water would already be out. My grandpa would run home, amazed: 'The pied one's back!' he'd keep shouting, 'Hilde, the pied one, I can't believe it.'

My grandma took my hand. 'No one knows how they manage to get home,' she told me. 'No matter where they set out from, they always get home – it's a miracle.'

The last pigeon slipped through the hatch and tumbled down between the others to the wooden trough. I'd have liked to know where it had been. My grandpa slowly got up from his stool and closed the hatch. His bones seemed tired. He poured the pigeons some fresh water. I realized I was freezing; the cold had crept into me as I'd been sitting still on the footstool. It was starting to get dark. We carefully went down the steps. My grandpa held my hand.

As soon as we were back, my grandma grabbed me in the hallway and pushed me into the bathroom. She turned on the tap, took my clothes off and rubbed my arms to warm them up. The water heater exuded a powerful warmth. I was shivering. 'Get in,' she said, 'so you don't catch a chill.'

After my bath, I wrapped a towel around my wet hair and looked in the mirror at the turban on my head. I wrapped myself in the big bath towel, leaving my shoulders and arms free, as women did after a shower. My grandma was cutting bread in the kitchen for supper, pressing it against her chest and sawing off slices with her breadknife. My grandpa was sitting at the table, and in front of him was the thick, well-worn book where he wrote his notes about the pigeons every evening. I glanced over his shoulder. His writing was small and spidery. I couldn't make out any of it. When I asked him what he was writing, he just shook his head absent-mindedly. Maybe my grandpa was jotting down which pigeon had been the last to return to the loft, or he was making a note of what he'd seen on the grizzle he'd picked up and held up to the light. Maybe he was giving the pigeons grades and marking them like in a class register. But that alone could never fill that many pages. The pigeon book must have been full of secrets my grandpa would never tell me, my grandma or anyone else in the world.

'Fashion show!' I shouted. My feet bare, I pranced back and forth in front of him and hummed a hit I'd heard on the radio. My grandpa looked up from his book and laughed. I held my head stiff so the turban wouldn't come apart, did a few circles and waved my arms around like wings. The bath towel slid to the floor. I picked it up and used it as a cloak, spreading it out with my arms, hoping it would float behind me like the train of a fairy's dress if I could just run round my grandpa fast enough. He watched my performance, amusement in his eyes, and he beckoned me closer. I shimmied over and stopped close to him, dancing on the spot. He leaned forward and looked at my chest. He narrowed his eyes, looked to the right, looked to the left, looked to the right again and finally slumped back into his chair and slapped his thigh enthusiastically with the palm of his hand. 'Our Tanja's growing a bust!' Walter said. I couldn't help but giggle and I felt my cheeks start glowing. Every now and then, when I'd stood in front of the mirror long enough, I'd imagined I could see two tiny bulges. But until now, no one else had confirmed it. I looked down at myself. If it was really starting, and my grandpa, looking at me happily, left it in no doubt, I'd be growing a real bosom, and with every child I had, that bosom would grow larger until it was as soft and sumptuous as my grandma's. I wrapped myself in the bath towel and wiggled my bottom as I walked to my bedroom. I turned around again and looked into my grandpa's proud, marvelling face.

*

Hildegard held the bulging shopping bag between her legs and her handbag on her lap. The vehicle rattled over the cobblestones. On the bend leading around the steelworks, Walter dropped his head onto Hildegard's shoulder. His hands slid off the handlebars. The vehicle slowly rolled into a concrete wall. Walter's head slid onto Hildegard's bosom from the impact. Milk spilled from the shopping bag onto the vehicle's floor. Hildegard threw open the passenger door. Walter slumped down on the bench seat, his wooden leg stretched out. If his eyes had been open, they couldn't have seen the pigeonless sky. Hildegard ran back and forth, away from the vehicle and then back to the vehicle. The milk dripped onto the road, trickling between the cobbles. 'Help!' she called, 'My Walter, the milk!' The barrier made its perky, steady sound. His heart had quite simply stopped.

WHAT CUSTOM STRICTLY DIVIDED

We're late. I underestimated how long the journey would take. Just knowing the way by heart doesn't make it any quicker.

I reach for Karl's hand, and we start running.

Karl is good at running, for his forty-eight years. He stretches forward with his thighs and plants his feet firmly on the ground; he grips the asphalt with his steps. Every movement is expansive. Karl doesn't mind having to exert himself, as long as there's a reason. And afterwards he doesn't mind being exhausted. He gasps, moans, winces, curses and laughs. 'The stage workhorse', they call him at the theatre, or sometimes 'the berserker'.

In the morning while the coffee's brewing, he'll sit at the table naked and light a cigarette. Karl uses his left hand to smoke. He flexes his right arm, holds his fist in front of his chest, sticks out his bottom lip and checks to see if his muscles still show on his upper arm. It's all about being strong, having a lust for life, grabbing it by the horns and getting down to it. First thing every morning, Karl wants to be sure he's still the same old Karl. He has no idea it's a foible of his. And I'm not going to tell him about it, because I don't want him to stop. Maybe later. We haven't known each other long.

I'm good at running too; after all I was still doing PE at school only a few months ago. But the baggy skirt I dug out for the day's festivities keeps getting caught on my tights; it's sticking to them and riding up. I should have left my harem pants on – they've passed every test so far.

We hurry up the shallow steps and weave our way through the hordes of people; we go through one of the smoked glass doors and feel the blast of warm air, pass the second set of doors and we're in.

But the journey doesn't end there; the Palace of the Republic is an enormous labyrinth. Looking up is especially bewildering: a thousand spherical lamps are hanging down in a chaotic system of various heights. It's not dazzling, but it certainly is bright. I've got lost here so many times, particularly when it's as full as it is now. Every year Beethoven's Ninth gets sold out weeks in advance: the most magnificent end to the year ever imaginable for Berlin's working masses. Father manages to get tickets somehow, without having to queue at the advance booking office; he always gets four just to be on the safe side. I only came along this time because I could bring Karl. I take him by the hand and lead him; I know the way to the cloakrooms – they're downstairs.

I can see the two of us in the mirrors covering the walls. Karl in his fur-lined denim jacket, which a colleague brought back for him from a tour in the West. He's grown so fond of it that he'll wear it until it falls off his shoulders in tatters. That'll be a sad day. Above his snuggly beige collar is Karl's gorgeous head – gorgeous, like people sometimes say about babies' heads. I can see his dark hair with the grey at his temples, his sturdy nose with its wondrous shape, his brown eyes – eyes that can blaze, eyes that glisten before tears overflow.

Next to Karl I'm glowing, with my red hair and red cheeks. My grandpa's coat is too wide at the shoulders, too long in the sleeves: a spacious refuge. Because of my caught-up skirt I'm taking small steps in my boots. Karl's walking purposefully in his trainers, although he doesn't know where he's going. He is completely focused. He doesn't know what my parents look like yet.

I've spotted them among the other guests. I force myself to breathe slowly. I search for the two of us in the mirror one last time and etch the image permanently into my mind – our image, the image of a beautiful, extraordinary couple.

'There they are,' I say.

Karl lets go of my hand. He's recognized them straight away. They're standing together, not saying a word; they've been waiting to take their seats for at least half an hour. Mother is deep in thought: her gaze – flickering between fear and an urge to dissect someone – might go unnoticed from a distance. Father's eyes rest steadily on us as we pant the last few feet.

'Hello,' I say, 'this is Karl, these are my parents.'

My voice breaks, as if I were standing in front of the class by the blackboard. I can no longer bring myself to say I'm sorry we're late. Karl holds out a hand to Mother.

'Good evening,' he introduces himself, 'Karl Kreuschler.'

He chuckles briefly because he's coming across so stiff and formal. No one reacts, not even me.

Mother has resolved to look beautiful and festive, but she's still doing that frantic flickering: her eyes flit from one point to another, never coming to a halt. She has her handbag clamped tight under her arm.

Father smiles dispassionately as he holds out his hand to Karl. He has a habit of pushing certain people away with his handshake. Sometimes he even does it with me. But today I don't even get a hello. Mother and Father are saying nothing. They would never admit they're angry.

Karl and I go to the cloakroom. I'd prefer to keep my coat on to hide my skirt, which is now sticking to my legs and revealing their shape in wavy crinkles. Mother's gaze lingers on them for a moment, and then she looks away to check the fit of her suit in the mirror. It has a subtle floral pattern and looks expensive. She probably bought it especially for tonight, like her shimmering silvery high heels which go with the suit. Mother and new shoes: her feet will already be suffering. Father stands tall in front of the mirror and adjusts his tie.

Now I can stop leading the way; no need to worry about a thing. With his back straight and his chin up, Father takes over the lead.

I can see the two of us in the mirrors covering the walls. Karl in his fur-lined denim jacket, which a colleague brought back for him from a tour in the West. He's grown so fond of it that he'll wear it until it falls off his shoulders in tatters. That'll be a sad day. Above his snuggly beige collar is Karl's gorgeous head – gorgeous, like people sometimes say about babies' heads. I can see his dark hair with the grey at his temples, his sturdy nose with its wondrous shape, his brown eyes – eyes that can blaze, eyes that glisten before tears overflow.

Next to Karl I'm glowing, with my red hair and red cheeks. My grandpa's coat is too wide at the shoulders, too long in the sleeves: a spacious refuge. Because of my caught-up skirt I'm taking small steps in my boots. Karl's walking purposefully in his trainers, although he doesn't know where he's going. He is completely focused. He doesn't know what my parents look like yet.

I've spotted them among the other guests. I force myself to breathe slowly. I search for the two of us in the mirror one last time and etch the image permanently into my mind – our image, the image of a beautiful, extraordinary couple.

'There they are,' I say.

Karl lets go of my hand. He's recognized them straight away. They're standing together, not saying a word; they've been waiting to take their seats for at least half an hour. Mother is deep in thought: her gaze – flickering between fear and an urge to dissect someone – might go unnoticed from a distance. Father's eyes rest steadily on us as we pant the last few feet.

'Hello,' I say, 'this is Karl, these are my parents.'

My voice breaks, as if I were standing in front of the class by the blackboard. I can no longer bring myself to say I'm sorry we're late. Karl holds out a hand to Mother.

'Good evening,' he introduces himself, 'Karl Kreuschler.'

He chuckles briefly because he's coming across so stiff and formal. No one reacts, not even me.

Mother has resolved to look beautiful and festive, but she's still doing that frantic flickering: her eyes flit from one point to another, never coming to a halt. She has her handbag clamped tight under her arm.

Father smiles dispassionately as he holds out his hand to Karl. He has a habit of pushing certain people away with his handshake. Sometimes he even does it with me. But today I don't even get a hello. Mother and Father are saying nothing. They would never admit they're angry.

Karl and I go to the cloakroom. I'd prefer to keep my coat on to hide my skirt, which is now sticking to my legs and revealing their shape in wavy crinkles. Mother's gaze lingers on them for a moment, and then she looks away to check the fit of her suit in the mirror. It has a subtle floral pattern and looks expensive. She probably bought it especially for tonight, like her shimmering silvery high heels which go with the suit. Mother and new shoes: her feet will already be suffering. Father stands tall in front of the mirror and adjusts his tie.

Now I can stop leading the way; no need to worry about a thing. With his back straight and his chin up, Father takes over the lead.

While she's walking beside him, Mother keeps turning her head. She looks at all the people, looks down, strokes the creases out of her suit, looks back at the people again. Father thinks she would be lost without him, with her underdeveloped sense of direction; she'd stray off and never get anywhere, ever. But Mother is fully occupied with something else: she's comparing herself with others. Wherever she is, she compares herself with others. She looks at where the women are looking. She wants to know if they're thinking what she thinks they're thinking. But here they're not thinking anything, they're just trying not to fall over as they take off their winter boots and put on their strappy sandals. They stretch their rear ends upwards with their knees together, leaning on their menfolk as there's nowhere to sit down here and nothing to hold on to.

Karl and I follow Mother and Father onto the escalator. We're standing three steps lower. Karl pulls his cigarettes and lighter out of his breast pocket. Much as I'd like one, I refrain from smoking. Mother and Father turn to us and see Karl having a drag. Aghast, they look away.

Karl tucks his cigarette into the corner of his mouth, and his shirt into his jeans. He could have borrowed a suit from the theatre's costume department for tonight – he doesn't own one himself. But he doesn't want to be forced into a suit if he's not working.

I touch Karl's right hand and quietly tell him I came here as a child to see *Little Bear's Dream*, and later, *Rock for Peace*. Karl laughs out loud.

'*Little Bear's Dream,*' he says and strokes my cheek with the back of two fingers.

Upstairs, Father walks past the bar and steps right up to the smoked glass windows. It's too late for a drink, but the obligatory gaze over the city can begin, unfortunately without a glass in hand this time: the Rotes Rathaus, the TV Tower, the Neptune Fountain, St Mary's Church, the Palace Hotel. Father adores observation decks and panoramic views. He gives the names of the most significant buildings and a few historical details; he knows his way around everywhere, no matter where he drags us: cities, landscapes, mountains, seas. The ex-geography-teacher's voice boldly speaks out from the army officer's mouth.

At home, Father will have considered putting on his dress uniform for tonight, like he did to my youth consecration four years ago. He far too rarely has an opportunity to show it off. The uniform is pale grey and has a narrow belt, cords across the chest and braided epaulettes, each with three stars. Every promotion brings one more star; four is the most you can have. The collar is trimmed with turquoise, and on the tips are two tiny silver aeroplanes, like you'd see in a toy shop.

Mother, as usual, will have deemed this outfit too ostentatious and talked Father out of wearing his dress uniform. So he's put on his dark grey double-breasted suit and a light-coloured shirt, along with his tie the shade of old roses. Now they don't stand out among all the other suits; they look a little above average, just the way Mother likes it.

Father turns away from the windows and struts towards the hall. Karl, who used the panoramic viewing time for a quick second cigarette, stubs it out in one of the ashtrays at the bar as he goes past. Who knows when he'll get his next one?

At the door to the hall, Father holds out the four tickets, carefully spread out like a fan in his hand. He gives the fan to the admissions lady. She puts them together and tears off a section from all of them at once. Father quickly gets his bearings and knows where our seats are. He lets Mother go first. She smiles shyly at the people, begging them with her eyes to stand up and let us through. Father thanks them, and Karl and I do the same. We sit in the order Father has in mind: Mother, Father, me, Karl.

Mother takes her glasses from their case and cleans them. As soon as she catches a snippet of conversation or a whiff of perfume, her frantic looking around starts all over again.

Father opens the programme. He studies the list of performers, looking for familiar names. Father is good at remembering names, especially famous ones. He mouths them over and over until he feels he knows them personally. He doesn't actually read the programmes, but he collects them in a pile on a bedroom shelf. After every concert or play, he writes the date on the front page and the names of who he was with. Father doesn't write the full names out; he uses abbreviations, preferably the first syllable of a name. Today he'll write '31.12.88, Si, Eck, Ta'. But what will he do with Karl? He can't write 'Karl', and he can't write 'Ka': he'd need to belong to the clan for that to happen. But he couldn't leave Karl out either; that would put the whole system into question. If Karl had a title of some sort, that would make things easier: 'Prof. Kreu'. An abbreviation like that would fit in nicely with 'Si, Eck, Ta'. But Karl doesn't have a title, and so it will come down to a disruptive 'Karl Kreuschler'. Father is and remains committed to the truth, but he finds ways to distance himself from it: '31.12.88, Si, Eck, Ta, Karl Kreuschler'.

'So many people,' I whisper to Karl.

'Yes,' says Karl, 'unbelievable.'

Karl wouldn't spend his New Year's Eve watching Beethoven's Ninth if it were down to him, and certainly not at the Palace. The Great Hall has the feel of a football stadium, a football stadium with a lid.

Everyone claps. Everyone takes a seat. The conductor raises his baton. Beethoven's Ninth begins.

Every year I wonder why the whole choir has to sit down right from the beginning, when they only actually sing at the end. A hundred people, sitting and sitting and sitting. When one of them stirs, I always hope they'll start singing, but no, an arm inconspicuously straightens, a score moves slightly in a hand, at most a foot changes position, and once again nothing happens. It must be terrible to stew in the limelight for almost an hour, unable to move. The first three movements are painfully long, meaningless and hateful; the choir is waiting, the soloists are waiting, thousands are waiting in the hall. We remain in a deathly stupor, letting the pompous sounds smother us, sweating silently under the Palace of the Republic's lid.

Beside me Karl sighs, a long breath from the depths of a downtrodden soul. I look into a face that's fighting time that does not want to go by. There is sweat on Karl's forehead.

'Tissue?' I ask quietly.

Karl nods. I lean towards Father, as he always has an opened packet of cellulose tissues in the inside pocket of his jacket. Karl grabs my arm and holds me back, shaking his head and briefly closing his eyes. He doesn't want it; he doesn't want a tissue from Father. He thought I had one myself. But I never remember tissues.

'OK?' I whisper.

'I'd rather be sitting by the aisle,' Karl whispers back.

I lay my hand on his; even the back of his hand is damp.

Here we go! Now! In perfect harmony, the choir jumps up from their chairs, precisely at the same time, as if they were puppets pulled up by invisible strings. How can it be that a hundred people can leap out of their torpor in one second flat, suddenly full of beans? This is the most wonderful moment in Beethoven's Ninth. I'd love to know how they do it.

The surprise echoes round the hall in murmurs. At last, the wait has paid off. The people wake up, straightening in their seats. Father tentatively drums along to the rhythm on his armrest but misses the beat. Mother's always laughing at him because he has no feeling for music. She moves to perch at the front of her seat, adjusting her glasses. Mother is in her element; she was a music teacher before she was made headteacher. Since then, she's lost the desire to make music, but she still holds on to a belief that she's musical.

'Freude, Freude, Freude,' the choir sings: joy, joy, joy. The famous motif already sounds full of promise. It's about to start, the 'Ode to Joy'. It is liberating, like a downpour flooding the hall after a drought. Anyone who's persevered to this point is about to be richly rewarded. Emotion, passion, pride; a universal elation seizes the people in the Palace of the Republic – goosebumps, lumps in throats, tears wiped away.

Those who have the privilege of being here are fortunate indeed.

Joy, beautiful spark of Divinity,
Daughter of Elysium,
We enter, drunk with fire,
Heavenly one, thy sanctuary!
Thy magic binds again
What custom strictly divided;
All people become brothers . . .

What custom strictly divided? What's that supposed to mean?

Mother with her custom of going out in high heels no matter how painful, me with my customary boots, Karl with his usual cigarettes and denim, even Father, fretting over his dress uniform and programme names – we're all meant to be brothers? No matter what we're accustomed to doing? We should simply be feeling joy – joy in the same place at the same time. Then the magic will happen. Then we can rejoice, entwined under the spark of Divinity. Mother, me, Karl and Father, in each other's arms, gently touched by the wings of the heavenly daughter. If we can just feel joy.

But what about? What can the four of us feel joy about at the same time and in the same place? We all feel joy about different things. I'm happy when the choir leaps up; Mother's happy that she knows the whole symphony off by heart; Father's happy to be here, and Karl will be happy to get out of here in one piece. I'm happy when Karl's naked, testing his biceps at the breakfast table; Karl's happy when I tell him about *Little Bear's Dream*; Father's happy when he can meet prominent personalities and shake their hand, and Mother will be happy if she manages not to see anyone she knows, now that she has Karl and me in tow.

Father's ignoring us. We're of no consequence to him, just like everything else that doesn't suit him or that he doesn't understand straight away. Mother, on the other hand, is ashamed of us. She's ashamed of me and ashamed of this man, this artist stinking of stale smoke who dares to come to the Palace in his threadbare jeans and worn trainers, without an ounce of respect for Beethoven's Ninth or the sumptuous ambiance, and who's managed to reel in this slip of a thing young enough to be his daughter.

This man, Karl Kreuschler, the most mild-mannered of actors, Karl, who rolls around on the floor with me, Karl, who hums me to sleep, Karl, in whose bear paws my face fits, is a smack in the face to Mother and Father.

'Bravo! Bravo! Bravo!' they're shouting. The hall erupts. The applause is thundering in my ears. The audience manages to outdo the choir's rejoicing at the end of the symphony. Joy, joy, joy. We rise from our seats. Father's clapping with his hands above his head, craning his neck to get a better view of the performers, shouting 'Bravo!' and again 'Bravo!' Mother beams at him, and now I feel ashamed. I look at Karl. He forces out a smile, half kind, half knowing, and looks away.

Outside, Father's taking care we don't get in other people's way as they're forcing their way out of the hall. He pushes Mother and me by our arms into a quiet corner that he's already earmarked for discussing our next move. I make the most of the high spirits that the music's aroused. Father's talking to me again. I've done my penance. He's working hard to restore his neutral expression, but I can see the residual moisture around his eyes; he tries to swallow his emotion and suggests going for a beer. He knows just the place. I nod.

'Oh yeah, a beer!' says Karl.

He's lit a cigarette and his right hand disappears into his trouser pocket; he shouldn't have sounded quite so keen. Mother smiles, a little sympathetically, but she is smiling.

'I'm still lost in the music,' she says.

Father turns to go. Downstairs I give him my cloakroom ticket and he takes his place in the queue. Mother, Karl and I wait by the mirrors.

The Palace experience is shorter than usual, and it's all down to me. Now I'm annoyed with myself for being late. While Father has his habit of circling the Glass Flower sculpture before the main event starts and immersing himself in the enormous socialist realist paintings hanging on the walls, I have a tradition of swiping a spoon, a knife, a cocktail glass – whatever comes to hand – from the foyer bar or the Linden restaurant. But today I won't have the opportunity. I already have a complete dinner set for two, including plates; what I'm still missing is coffee cups. It's not just me – all my friends have prized pieces with the squiggly 'PdR' monogram in their kitchen cupboards, and even families from the provinces who take a trip to the capital manage to stash away a cake fork at least. There's no better souvenir from the iconic building than one acquired in this way. Over the years it's developed into a secret national sport; at home, people show one another their treasures and tell each other funny stories of how they came about them.

Behind my father's rigid back as he devoutly studies the artworks by Willi Sitte and Lothar Zitzmann, the Palace is emptying its own temple: the masses are neatly and fairly dividing the inventory among themselves. And without so much as a murmur, a never-ending source quietly replenishes the stock of plates, glasses and spoons.

Father gives Karl his jacket and helps Mother into her coat. I slip mine on. Father holds the door open for us. In pairs we go left, walk around the Palace and cross the bridge over the Spree. Mother has her arm in Father's; I think I can detect a limp in her steps.

Karl drags on his cigarette and blows white clouds into the cold. My hand looks for his, finds it and is wrapped in five warm fingers and one hot palm.

Father turns around, but not to us. We follow his gaze, back, up, towards the Palace, clashing with the darkness with its sharp edges, grandiose and dazzlingly bright, making the first New Year's fireworks over the city look like tired, blinking fireflies.

'Erich's lamp shop,' mutters Karl, repeating the classic old Palace joke.

We reach the Nikolaiviertel, Berlin's newest showpiece, the reconstructed old quarter.

Father heads off to a spot he has in mind for a drink – the Gerichtslaube. The four of us push our way through the entrance, blocking the inner door; that's as far as we can get. At the tables, at the bar, in the aisles, everywhere, there are well-dressed people with glazed expressions and paper hats. The waitress is winding her way through the crush, balancing her tray of beers high above her head; it almost touches the garlands hanging from the ceiling.

We go back out onto the street. Father knows another bar not far from here – the Nussbaum. We'll try that one. But at the entrance we are bombarded with the sound of laughter, background music, a blue haze and high-spirited people shouting into each other's ears. No room for us.

There's nothing to be had in the Nikolaiviertel without a reservation, especially not on New Year's Eve. But Father's not giving up; we set off towards the Rippe. Karl and I straggle along behind the two of them over the medieval cobbles. Father's striding through the history-soaked air around the St Nicholas Church; Mother's stumbling as she gets her heels caught between the smooth, round stones.

We step into the hopelessly overcrowded Rippe, but this time Father pushes a path through for us. He stoops to speak to the sweating waiter, and the waiter nods curtly. We jostle behind Father; we're stuck here, two, three metres from the entrance, and this is where we're staying. Karl and Father are standing three people deep from the bar with their backs to it; Mother and I have the backrests of two chairs prodding into our bottoms, and every now and then the heads of the lucky people sitting on them press into the smalls of our backs. No point in even thinking of taking our coats off; Mother would have more chance of putting both her legs in the air and shaking out her aching feet without falling over. Although we haven't ordered yet, the waiter reaches through the crowd and passes us four glasses of beer, froth dripping down their sides: two large for Father and Karl, two small ones for Mother and me.

'Good health,' says Father.

'Cheers,' says Karl.

I raise my glass and it makes a dull clink against Mother's, Father's and Karl's. We drink, not just from thirst but, more than anything, to be rid of the extra ballast as soon as possible. Mother finds it hard to drink so quickly; some froth has run down her coat, her hand's wet and every time the stranger's head pushes into her back, she looks round with a stern expression before turning back, widening her eyes and searching for allies to join her in her reproach – in Father and in me, but not in Karl, who's just making everything even worse; he's lit a cigarette and can't work out where to blow the smoke nor where to put his ash.

'So you're an actor,' asks Father.

'Yes,' says Karl, puffing out his smoke above everyone's heads.

'Here in Berlin?' asks Father.

He simply doesn't believe it, or at any rate he thinks there's a huge catch, as the name Karl Kreuschler doesn't ring any bells for him. The moment he first reads Karl's name in some programme or other, he'll have to think again.

'Since September, at the Volksbühne,' says Karl.

Mother takes a break from pretending to be interested in Karl by sipping from her beer glass. Father looks at me.

'And what are you doing there now?' he asks.

'I sit in on the rehearsals.'

Father grins. He takes a big gulp of beer.

'You make the coffee,' he says.

'I watch.'

My words turn to dust in Father's ears.

'Observing and writing descriptions, that's what she does,' says Karl.

Karl's rescuing me. I'll always be grateful to him for that.

'Rehearsal notes,' I say, because it sounds impressive.

Mother nervously pulls up the collar of her coat.

'Tanja's good, she helps us, it's the only way to learn,' says Karl.

'Learn what?' asks Father.

'How theatre works,' says Karl.

Karl's beautiful eyes have lit up and are ablaze. This horrifies Mother, who looks over to Father's face to borrow some of his superiority. Father doesn't say what he's thinking: that artistic types spend their nights drinking themselves stupid and whoring to excess. But he still manages to let us know his feelings on the subject.

'So I presume you've given up on your studies,' Father asks me.

'Well, not necessarily, but qualifications won't be enough on their own,' says Karl.

Our glasses are empty, apart from Mother's. Father takes it out of her hand. He opens his mouth like a beak, tips the last of the beer into it and pays.

Outside, Mother waves her coat about to shake off the smell. Father pushes Karl away with a handshake and smiles dispassionately.

'Thanks for inviting me,' says Karl.

Father doesn't react. He holds out a hand to me. I put mine in it. He squeezes it, reminding me I'm wearing a ring.

'Goodbye, happy New Year,' Mother says to Karl.

'Oh yeah, happy New Year,' Karl says and laughs.

'Bye,' says Mother, and she pulls me towards her with one hand, fleetingly strokes me with the other and gives me a look whose meaning not even she knows.

'Keep in touch,' Father then says.

They head off to the S-Bahn station. They have to go to Marzahn, to celebrate with one of Father's colleagues. I wonder how Mother will manage to reach the New Year in those heels. They'll be taking a taxi home.

Karl takes my hand. We start walking aimlessly, in the opposite direction.

'Give us one,' I say.

Karl stops. He takes his cigarettes out of his breast pocket. I take one from the pack, as does Karl. His hand shields the flame as he lights them.

I go to take his hand and start walking again; what my fingers find is a teaspoon marked 'PdR'. I laugh out loud at Karl's boyish grin.

'Where did you get that from?' I ask.

'My first,' says Karl.

We decide not to take the bus. We'd rather walk to the theatre; it's only half past nine.

'How does *Little Bear's Dream* go, then?' asks Karl.

I inhale the scent of Karl's skin. I kiss him on the mouth. I bury my face in his fur collar.

'I can't remember.'

Karl runs his bear paw through my hair.

'None of it?'

'Well, he did have a really big head.'

Karl chuckles, snorts, wheezes.

'They'll be saying you're old enough to be my father,' I say.

Karl takes my face in his hands. He strokes my eyebrows with his thumbs. His fingers almost reach the nape of my neck.

'But I'm not,' he says, 'but I'm not.'

SEVENTY-TWO STEPS

I started counting from the kerbstone on the corner of Drieselstrasse. That was where Nina and I had picked up the lame sparrow. We'd wrapped it in Nina's scarf so only its head was peeking out and we carefully carried it home. After that, whenever I walked in this direction, I'd count my steps from the Drieselstrasse kerb to number twenty-eight, where Nina lived.

There were seventy-two, and I wondered why I'd never talked to Nina about it. She knew nothing about it whatsoever. It was always seventy-two steps. That meant I must have been grown up for an eternity. I'd reached my final height and stride many years before and yet I still felt as if I'd just turned twelve.

I opened the front door; it made a louder creak than ever. There was a dog turd halfway up the stairs, no doubt from Herr Schlemm-Heise's fleabag. Either it or its owner hadn't made it to the street in time. The house had become more and more run down.

Nina led me into the red 'salon', as she called the room that had once been the children's bedroom, pursing her lips as she did so. Two weeks earlier she'd bought a new carpet, soft and deep red, which had already lost its shape and now formed waves across the empty room. I pushed one of the waves with the tip of my toe to smooth it down. But the velvety floor didn't give way; it was as if it had been poured in and solidified.

'You can move your things in here,' Nina said.

Nina came into the kitchen with two of the good glasses. She uncorked the wine bottle and asked when Benno was coming, and if he knew already.

'Oh, Benno,' I said. 'Benno's coming by train tomorrow afternoon, at two forty-three, unless anything changes.'

He didn't know I'd broken up with Karl the night before. I definitely had to call Benno later.

Nina's kitchen table was cluttered with so many useless things. Everything she'd ever taken from the cupboard or brought into the room had been pushed to one side after she'd used it. I could get a rough idea of what might have gone on here recently from this collection of paraphernalia: four teaspoons (licked clean), an opened bulk pack of aspirin plus vitamin C, three paper umbrellas which had once adorned ice cream sundaes, an almost empty honey jar missing its lid, Nina's library card, two packets of dextrose sweets, a small cuddly cow, its front hooves hugging the trunk of a money plant whose plump leaves were covered in a layer of dust, five blunt pencils, a sample-sized bottle of perfume, soy sauce, a dozen coloured glass beads, a theatre 'What's On' leaflet from the previous month, a takeaway pizza flyer, a half-full bottle of rum and two lighters, probably empty.

The remaining third of the tabletop was taken up by the ashtray, the wine glasses and our elbows. I suspected this area would keep shrinking day by day. We'd sooner have moved to the table in the living room than clear the decks properly in here: Nina, because she'd come to terms with the chaos and had more important things to do, and me, because I'd just left a flat where, through my constant tidying and cleaning, free space had finally been achieved. I felt violated by the mess, like I'd been set back light years, and it seemed that the only way to endure my failure was to ignore it as a matter of principle.

We finished the bottle, and I picked up another one from the corner shop over the road. When I came back, Nina started talking about the future, or at any rate the future we had in common, and just the very near future. She said we'd get up the next morning and have breakfast, then make the red salon cosy; her parents' old suitcases were in the corridor halfway up the stairs and we could use them to pick up all my things from Karl's apartment at some point later; there was no hurry, she could lend me anything until then. The next day she'd ask Jeff, her actor boyfriend, to bring the mattress over from his apartment, seeing as he either slept with her or didn't sleep at all.

When we'd emptied the second bottle of wine, I suddenly realized what it was that made Nina different from everyone else: she couldn't ever see the grand scheme of things, but she had a talent for picking out from the chaos the exact detail she'd need next so it never descended on her completely. She didn't make her way through life with flying colours, but she pushed through step by step with her head down; and now she was pushing through for the both of us. She could fiddle with something tiny she'd stumbled upon for hours – I once saw her polishing her grandmother's silverware – and be so engrossed that she'd spin an imaginary cocoon around herself while outside the world was falling apart. This was how Nina survived every maelstrom. Actually, that was something we always had in common: our aversion to the big picture.

Although my tongue felt swollen and was sticking to the roof of my mouth, I reached for the rum. At that moment, I understood that Nina's overloaded kitchen table was nothing more than a metaphor for the whole apartment, which uncomplainingly held all its former inhabitants' clutter, amassed in layers: an apartment where I might live, but where I'd never be at home.

'Weren't you going to call Benno?' Nina asked.

She yawned. I picked myself up from the table and said Benno's mobile phone number out loud: zero-one-seven-two-seven-two-two-eight-one-four-four. Yes, now I was in the right mood to confront Benno with the catastrophe.

'Benno Beyer, Tutti-Frutti Ice Cream Institute, how can I be of service?'

'I broke up with Karl last night. Because of you.'

Benno went quiet. I could have seen that coming. I took a sip of the rum I'd brought from the kitchen. Benno had gone quiet because he wanted to avoid what I'd said. It was like hanging up, only more expensive at sixty pfennigs a minute. Other people might have taken up vast amounts of speaking time they weren't entitled to, but it was silence that Benno claimed for himself, and that seemed even more presumptuous. All I could hear was a windy hissing.

By the time I'd given up on Benno, the entire apartment was dark. Nina had gone to bed. I wanted to go to the bathroom, but I couldn't find the light switch. As I groped my way into the bedroom, I bumped into a cupboard door that had been left open. It made a bang. I rubbed my forehead.

I crawled into Nina's bed, as Jeff usually did, into the bed her father had built himself from wood – the same bed we'd pulled bloody sheets off all those years before. Nina rubbed my back until I fell asleep.

Benno stood in the bedroom doorway, in a long cashmere coat, with his dark-rimmed doe eyes. The shirt he was wearing under his coat had a green and red checked pattern which looked like the covers on Nina's feather duvet. Nina appeared in a bathrobe, half-asleep, behind Benno. It was only half past nine. She must have let him in. How had he got here so quickly?

Benno pulled up the corners of his mouth and brows in an attempt to rouse some happiness and energy, and he pressed a bulging tote bag into Nina's hand. He threw a two-kilo illustrated book bearing the title *The Battle of the Sexes* to me on the green and red checked duvet. He opened his shabby leather bag, and with a little effort he took out a fax machine.

'What's this?' Nina asked.

She had unpacked the tote bag and was kneeling in front of a package of fresh sausages the size of a car battery. Benno didn't say a word; he made his way to the nearest socket to test out the fax machine. I got out of bed; I didn't know what to do with the coffee table book. Benno explained to Nina that if she wanted to open her casting agency to get work for him and Jeff, the first thing she'd need was a fax machine.

Nina looked at me. As I wasn't about to offer any help, she stared at the pack of sausages again and picked it up.

'I'll make breakfast first,' she said, disappearing into the kitchen.

Benno didn't steal like Nina did: back in the days before the Wall came down, it had been fifteen-pfennig fizzy drink powder; now it was a fourteen-marks-ninety-nine mascara. But Benno had always stolen on a grand scale: tastefully, originally and in a way that made it worth it. I tried to estimate the value of what he'd brought: the sausages forty marks, the book eighty, the fax machine five hundred; Benno had come here with over six hundred marks in kind. He looked after Nina and me with the affectionate care of a tomcat laying dead mice by his owner's door at night. In a way, these gifts were a sign he was putting his feet under the table. They expressed his desire to be there with us, and as it turned out later, they were his contribution towards the monthly rent of just under nine hundred marks. Benno didn't say a word about Karl, about me, about us.

'And the coat?' I asked.

'Seven hundred marks.'

The man who had paid in front of him at Peek & Cloppenburg had been inattentive, slow and just the same height as Benno, so he took the bag as it was looking lonely on the counter.

Benno laughed. Then he spread out his arms; I went over to him and he enveloped me. I was transfixed.

'I feel so bad for Karl,' I heard Benno whisper. I swallowed.

'Me too.'

Benno worshipped Karl. He'd seen him on stage twice and on TV once, and at night he made me tell him the five fabulous tales I'd memorized from Karl's thirty-two years in acting, over and over again, so he could rid himself of the doubts that had plagued him since he'd passed his drama school test two weeks earlier. Of course, I worshipped Karl too. I still adored him, even then, and more than ever since two nights before, when I'd uttered those words at forty-nine minutes past midnight.

I remembered the boots I'd recently bought Karl. Black lace-up boots, lined, size forty-three, costing sixty-nine marks. It was already a harsh winter, but Karl, stubborn and incorrigible, was still going around in trainers. They'll be the death of you, I'd said for the umpteenth and final time. I knew full well Karl would never wear those boots.

The bell rang. Jeff was standing at the door with the mattress. He asked where exactly he was meant to sleep now.

'Well, with me, of course! Breakfast's ready,' Nina said.

She'd taken all the clutter off the table and put it on the windowsill and the dresser. Jeff, Benno and I stood around the table where four red candles had been lit, and variations of sausage were decorated with paper umbrellas, waiting to be eaten.

'Is it a special occasion?' Jeff asked.

He always forgot birthdays, so was on the defensive. He put on the expression he'd practised for moments like these, looking out from behind his unkempt hair with hangdog eyes. But none of us had a birthday that day. I'd be next on 20 February; on 4 June it would be Karl's turn, then Benno on 15 July, then Nina on 8 August, and in almost a year it would be Jeff's, who had just turned twenty-six, on 3 November.

'We're now almost a kind of commune,' Nina said, solemnly raising her coffee cup.

We toasted each other and sat down: Jeff, who seemed so tiny next to Benno, in the furthest corner on the orange plastic stool, Nina and Benno on the wooden chairs from the living room and me in the fifties armchair, which was much too low for the table, but otherwise very comfortable. We instinctively kept this seating arrangement; from that day on, 19 November, which was a Tuesday, we each had at least one set place among the chaos.

'I'm going to the cinema,' Nina said.

She often spent her evenings at the cinema: three times a week, usually alone. Jeff didn't have time for cinema; he was invariably rehearsing, and always for a problematic project. He'd catch the last U-Bahn at one fifty-three, sleep by Nina's side for five and a half hours, throw his clothes on in the morning, wash down two aspirin plus vitamin C tablets with a black coffee and rush out of the door.

Nina wanted to work in the film industry. As a production assistant or a unit manager, she always said. At the moment, no one wanted to employ her so she just went to the movies. It was her way of keeping abreast of what was happening in the industry and a chance to immerse herself in a darkened world where she could relinquish any responsibility for two hours and get high on emotions.

When Nina did have film jobs, she was the same as Jeff: she'd work on production for sixteen hours a day and would only come home to sleep. I had no idea what exactly Nina did in those sixteen hours. If I asked her about it, she'd answer me with a mixture of technical terms and emotional words, and I might grasp it for a moment before it escaped me again.

Nina asked me if I wanted to go with her to the cinema, but I just shook my head, and anyway she knew I'd be waiting for Benno. I was always waiting for Benno because he never let anyone know when he'd arrive. When he did arrive, I always made sure to blame him for wasting my time. Though, truthfully, I spent about nine hours a day showering, doing the shopping, talking on the phone and reading the paper.

Nina zipped up her boots, put her key in her coat pocket and wrapped her scarf around her neck two and a half times. She gave me a kiss and opened the door. There was Benno, standing on the threshold. Nina gave a start and rolled her eyes. Benno, the eternal surprise guest, could become exhausting over time.

'Herr Schlemm-Heise's doing his water-skiing in the entrance,' Benno said.

He had to mime it three times before it dawned on us what he meant. Herr Schlemm-Heise, our neighbour who was severely lacking in both social skills and good health, had always owned a German shepherd. The relationship between the two of them had evolved over the last six years to the extent that now the dog would take its master out for a walk, and at a good twenty kilometres per hour. Herr Schlemm-Heise would stiffen up and brace his whole body against the dog's pull – that was how he managed to keep his speed down, if only a little, on the slippery hall tiles.

'The trailers will have started,' Nina said, running down the stairs.

Benno let me pull him into the red salon. We undressed and lay down on Jeff's mattress. This was the moment I was always waiting for; the moment that justified my miserable state of affairs. Benno's hands engulfed my body, one area after another, and I wouldn't have minded disappearing into those hands, never to be seen again.

Jeff's mattress consisted of three sections, which only gave an impression of staying together when they were enclosed in fitted sheets. If I was alone and drunk, I'd fall into a deep sleep on this construction and I'd wake up at ten the next morning without having moved a muscle. But when Benno was with me, we were constantly moving and the three sections would slip apart straight away without any resistance. We'd push them back together about forty times a night. Initially this battle just encouraged us; after all, it was a Sisyphean task which required athletic perseverance, profound lust and shamelessness. But time and time again we'd start our nights on the three sections, only to roll onto the red carpet after a high-spirited warm-up, where we would carry on with our lovemaking between two carpet waves colliding at an obtuse angle. I developed a secret theory that possessing something intact to sleep on would herald the end of the relationship. It was a lazy excuse to not get a real bed. After three of those nights in a row with Benno, I began to doubt that an intact relationship was preferable to an intact mattress. Karl and I had bought a king-sized futon. In time, I began to resent Benno for bringing packs of sausage and fax machines instead of a real bed.

Benno whispered something in my ear and lifted himself off me. I regretted that, because even when exhausted, he still made a magnificent blanket. He crawled back onto the three sections on all fours, let himself drop and fell asleep. I could have squeezed in with him for a while, to get warm and keep him from nodding off, but fifteen minutes on that mattress with him would have been enough. So I gave up and spread the sleeping bag out on the hard floor so at least one of us would have the chance to recuperate.

Benno was breathing evenly and noisily; each breath took him four seconds. Not a twitch crossed his face. His long legs hung over the edge of the mattress, and the covers were half a metre too short for him. I shrank Benno down in my mind's eye and imagined him in his mother's arms with his head heavy and his limbs hanging limply, fallen asleep before she could put him to bed.

I thought of opening the window for some fresh air, and realized it was something I'd never done since I'd moved into the red salon. So I left it and sat motionless on the carpet.

I was glad when I heard Nina put the key in the lock and open the door at half past midnight. I pulled on my bathrobe and went into the hallway.

'Let's put the light on,' I said, pressing the switch by the door. Nina stood there blinking as if she'd been caught out. She came in from the cold with a red nose and swollen eyes.

'Oh my,' I said.

I turned the light off again straight away. Nina had to laugh.

'Beautiful film. Can't put it into words.'

In the kitchen, I lit a candle from the pack of ten. Then I opened the wine. Nina was freezing and sniffling. I wrapped her in the duvet from her bedroom and sat her in the fifties armchair. Nina drew her legs up. She hid her face in the quilt because she was ashamed to be crying in front of me. She waved her hand in the air to ask me to stop looking at her. And even though the duvet cover was getting wetter and wetter, I could hear Nina giggling. She was giggling and sobbing all at the same time into the green and red checks. When she tried to say something, only a squeak came out of her; she'd lost her voice. She was seized by a fresh wave of emotion, which sent her back and forth between gurgling with laughter and sniffling. It had always been like that; Nina could cry the most enormous tears, for the longest time. I would have liked to cry along with her, but never could. At least I could giggle. I clinked my glass against hers, which stood untouched on the table.

I went to the pharmacy – might it actually represent the exact midpoint between the Drieselstrasse kerb where we'd first found the lame sparrow, in other words my step zero, and our entrance at number twenty-eight, in other words my seventy-second step? That would justify its existence, at last. If so, it would be exactly thirty-six steps to our front door if I started counting from the pharmacy. I'd have to check on the way back.

'Twenty-eight fifty,' said the woman behind the till, keeping her face neutral. I wasn't sure if it was her normal expression or one reserved for pregnancy tests: she had no way of knowing what result I was hoping for. The test seemed really expensive to me. Maybe we could agree on a half-price deal if it turned out positive? But then again, even fourteen marks twenty-five was too much to pay for bad news.

On the way back, the German shepherd raced past me with Herr Schlemm-Heise. I never knew that Herr Schlemm-Heise was such an early riser. When I got back to the apartment, the others were still sleeping peacefully; it was only eight twenty-two.

I locked myself in the toilet. I'd spent the night before dividing the twenty-eight-day cycle by two, then calculating the length of time around ovulation when I was able to conceive and putting the results into context, first with my diary and then with my head, to allow for a modicum of hope. I read the leaflet twice. Don't want to make a mistake at this point. Stream of pee. One red line. Four minutes. Two red lines. Of course. I knew it.

I stared at the two red lines for thirty seconds, and then I went to the kitchen and filled the sink. Time for the mountain of dirty dishes. Sometimes I really liked washing up. I tried not to clatter too much and wake the others.

The eleven glasses, seven cups, ten plates, six knives, two forks, two large and five small spoons were clean. All that remained was a chopping board, three encrusted saucepans and two frying pans. Before I set to work on the bigger items, I had to make room. I took a tea towel from the hook next to the sink. The first glass slipped out of my fingers and shattered on the floor. I'd finish washing up first and clear the shards up afterwards. The second glass must have been a particularly delicate one: it broke in my hands. I gave up and dragged the vacuum cleaner from the bathroom into the kitchen and hoovered up the mess, criss-crossing the space in front of me without a method, distracted by the loud noise.

Jeff roared over the din to ask what was wrong with me. I saw him standing in the doorway in crumpled boxers. I roared back to ask if he didn't have a rehearsal that morning.

'Crisis meeting at twelve,' Jeff roared again.

Then he went to the bathroom. I turned off the vacuum cleaner and made coffee. Nina came in, sighed and swept up the remains of the broken glass. She grabbed a cup and held it towards the coffee pot. I poured her a coffee and told her. When Benno showed up, I told him too. Then he turned on his heel and was gone. When Jeff finally came out of the bathroom, I said it for the third time to complete the picture. We sipped our coffee, and Jeff rolled a cigarette for me. The front door slammed shut. Benno probably needed some fresh air. Jeff sloped off into the living room. Nina looked at me. I must have been biting my lower lip for twenty minutes: it was bleeding.

I was the last to leave the apartment.

I began counting at the front door. By the Drieselstrasse kerb, I'd reached seventy-two steps. It was reassuring that it worked the other way around too. I carried on counting until I was at one hundred and sixty-seven, at the corner of Brehmestrasse. Just counting wasn't much of a challenge on its own, so I decided not to step on the cracks between the paving slabs. As a result, I had to either shorten or lengthen my stride. I decided to shorten it. Walking became teetering. At three hundred and thirty-five I was at Talstrasse. If I wanted to go to Karl's – and that was precisely what I wanted – I now had to take the gravel path across Bürgerplatz. But that was out of the question: the gravel path had no slabs and no cracks to not step on. I had to make a detour. I turned into Talstrasse. I stepped up the challenge and resolved to get to Karl's only by taking pavements with slabs and cracks, with no exceptions. If I wanted to cross a road, it couldn't be tarmacked; only cobblestones would do for me. I reached Sonnenburger Strasse at six hundred and three. I had to admit that I'd already broken the rules four times and made excuses for the toe of one of my shoes which had clearly touched the crack between two slabs. I gave step-counting priority over the ban on cracks, but I came up with a punishment to avoid becoming careless: if I came into contact with a gutter, even once, I wasn't allowed to go to Karl's, and that was that. I just had to make an effort. What were my piffling troubles compared to the state Karl was in? I didn't even want to think about it. Stunned by my abrupt departure, Karl was sitting on the sofa every night, smoking cigarette after cigarette, drinking beer after beer, schnapps after schnapps, and with the alcohol concentrating in his blood, the water in him would rise and rise until it reached his head and could finally flow from his eyes.

It happened. With the ball of my foot, I'd landed in a gutter filled in with cement. The line had been crossed. There was no hiding from it. I'd lost my concentration, and now it was time to pay for it. I'd been sloppy and I had to take the consequences. My chance was gone, once and for all.

I stood in the middle of a square stone slab. The streets here were called An der Kolonie and Ahornweg. I'd wandered into an area I wasn't familiar with. Where should I go now? The only people I could think of were my parents. They wouldn't be home before five o'clock anyway, in two and a half hours at the earliest. I had enough time for twenty or thirty detours. I pulled myself together. I couldn't afford to make another mistake. First, I had to manoeuvre my way out of this alien cul-de-sac. I cautiously turned a hundred and eighty degrees on the stone square. With my eyes fixed on the cracks, I teetered off again. I had to get back to a place I knew my way around. From there, I'd work out a new battle plan to lead me to my parents: not a direct route but one that followed the rules. I forced myself to slow down and place my feet carefully. The paving slabs were lined up evenly and consistently. I set off at a good pace. It was going well for me. Later, when I arrived at my parents', I'd eat every single thing my mother put on my plate. I skirted a patch of footpath covered in tarmac. I had to watch out for traps like that. I couldn't shake off the suspicion that I was moving further and further away from everything I knew. I wasn't able to check: it would have been reckless to raise my head and look around. Four elongated slabs, contrary to the usual size and laid at a later date, made me stumble. At the last moment, I jumped to the right onto a square slab and clung to the wall of a house. I'd avoided disaster by a hair's breadth. Why hadn't I seen the hazard in time? I was shaken. The sun was already going down. It would be dark by half past four. I summoned all my strength and squinted. All I wanted to see was cracks. I was obsessed. If I could just keep going, I'd have mulled wine to look forward to: glühwein from litre tetrapaks which my father would eagerly heat and top up, pleased I'd dropped by. I swore to myself that I'd drown the fertilized egg clinging on in my belly like a parasite in that glühwein.

Despite the darkness, the cracks appeared more clearly before my narrowed eyes, as if I'd tamed them. They made themselves known to me; yes, they were obeying me, becoming wider and blacker, and now they were standing out quite clearly from the slabs. Discipline and perseverance were paying off. I had overcome every obstacle. I had broken the cracks' resistance. Above the milky grey footpath, at ankle height, a dense network of thick, black lines was floating up for me to climb through.

It was Wednesday 11 December when I entered the apartment at ten thirty-six. Jeff was standing on the scales in the bathroom – he claimed he'd put on three kilos over the last seven days just because of all the lebkuchen he'd eaten. Nina stroked Jeff's belly and asked where I'd been.

'For a walk,' I said.

I took off my coat and shoes and stepped on the scales. Out of the three of us, I was the heaviest at sixty-five kilos, but now the needle was pointing to seventy-one. So my body was already depositing reserves to protect the unborn life within it. Six kilograms for a five-millimetre embryo – if this carried on, what would I look like in two weeks, in two months? A ball of fat on legs: that was what I was. Where was Benno anyway? On the way to the phone, I saw a bag in the hallway. I didn't recognize it; I couldn't remember shopping anywhere. Unpack the bag first, then call Benno, I told myself. I'd still be able to get on his nerves later.

A two-kilo net of tangerines, two thirty-centimetre chocolate Father Christmases and three litres of glühwein in tetrapaks. I carried it all into the kitchen and put it in the bottom of the four-door dresser, glad no one had seen me doing it – Nina and Jeff had gone back to bed. I opened the fridge. Two packs of egg salad and a piece of cheese came towards me. The fridge was jam-packed: Benno had struck again. I tried to close the door, but twice it sprang open. The third time, I slammed it shut with all my strength. Apart from some Kinder eggs and the ketchup bottle, everything inside slid towards me in a kind of chain reaction. Pregnant women were supposed to have a contented look about them, but I seemed to be debilitated. I sorted the cartons, cans and packets by weight and size and stacked them back in the fridge. When I was thirty, I calculated, my child would be six; when I was forty, it would be sixteen; when I was fifty, it would be twenty-six. Try again, not with force but with feeling, I said to myself, and carefully pressed the fridge door shut. It stayed shut. I had to go to a gynaecologist to ask for an abortion, the very next day – at eight o'clock sharp. But how did you go about doing that? The bell rang. One minute past eleven. I ran to the door. Benno came in, his leather bag under his arm.

'No one in?' he asked quietly. I nodded towards the closed bedroom door. Benno tiptoed into the red salon, closed the door and sat down on the floor, bag in hand. I sat down opposite him, cross-legged, five centimetres separating our knees. Benno pulled out a brick-sized package in a grey cardboard sleeve and gave it to me. I took off the cover. It was a brand-new bible: one thousand, one hundred and fifty-eight pages of Old Testament, three hundred and twenty-five of New. As I began to leaf through the pages, I asked Benno where he'd found it.

'It's not what you think. Read to me,' Benno said, laying his head in my lap.

At eleven o'clock at night, Jeff was standing outside the front door, a crowd gathered behind him.

'Party,' Jeff said.

He kissed Nina, and then, while I held the door open, thirty-four people walked past me and evenly dispersed into the rooms. Nina and I didn't bother to question it; we went into the kitchen, cobbled together a cold buffet from what was to hand and carried the plates, bowls and platters to the table in the living room. Among the hungry were actors, drama students and people from film and theatre who, as they ate, all began to seem confusingly alike. The buffet was gone in ten minutes, and even the two chocolate Father Christmases disappeared without a trace. The music was booming, and Nina and I dashed out of the kitchen with open wine bottles and back with empty ones; we filled the fridge with beer cans and set out eight saucers to serve as ashtrays.

'Well, you're having a smashing party. Can I come in?'

Poor Herr Schlemm-Heise was standing in the hall – poor because his dog had bitten his nose off. It had happened a fortnight before, and now it was sewn back on with twelve clearly visible stitches, sitting intact in the middle of his face again, swollen to the size of a hen's egg and a shade of reddish-violet. We danced around Herr Schlemm-Heise and nudged him towards the living room; on the way he showed how eager he was for some fun by flexing his arms and wiggling his hips. Nina removed a couple dressed in black from the ancient leather armchair and sat him down. I realized I hadn't seen Benno since the horde had descended on us an hour and a half earlier.

'Cultural programme for Herr Schlemm-Heise!' I shouted twice.

Benno fell into the trap straight away and emerged from the bedroom – my call had worked. Behind him I could see two girls with big eyes: a blonde who must have weighed less than fifty kilos and one with long, black hair who looked like she had an eating disorder. Benno announced that he'd tried to get the Czech singer Karel Gott's phone number from international directory enquiries on his mobile phone, but he'd only got as far as the Prague area code. The girls giggled, and I could see Benno was showing his best side to his future fellow students.

With the same determination, he now wanted to prove his talent to Herr Schlemm-Heise. Benno took the antenna off the plastic Berlin TV Tower, a dusty seventies souvenir from Nina's parents, and used his new microphone to offer our guests an exclusive Karel Gott medley. Not only did he know all the tunes: Benno could also remember all the lyrics of 'Biene Maja', 'Weisst du wohin' and 'Du bist da für mich' off by heart. He had Gott's Czech accent down to a T, as well as his spirited knee-twitching and the way he switched his mic impulsively from one hand to the other and back. He topped off the performance by stretching out his hand, caressing the heavens, with his gaze fixed far off up into the distance. Benno's audience cheered, and I found myself thinking that if Karl had been there, he might have got carried away with an Elvis medley. But Karl wasn't there, and Benno suddenly had to cut short his performance to run to the bathroom.

Jeff fell to his knees in front of me, holding on to my leg. When I shouted that he'd got me mixed up with Nina and that she was in the kitchen, he sat up and begged, let out a bark and bit me on the thumb. I fled to Nina at the kitchen table.

'It's never been so crowded in here,' I said.

'Yes it has – remember the night you lost your virginity?' Nina said.

We'd invited our class and a few of the gang round because Nina was turning fifteen and her parents were on a business trip. I felt my face turning red. That party ten years earlier had been touchingly innocent compared to this one, apart from my crush on the boy with muscles from the neighbouring school – even Nina had forgotten his name – whom I was convinced I had to help with his maths. And what I'd started had to be taken to its conclusion, the whole thing ending in a lengthy, painful procedure on the wooden bed in Nina's parents' gloomy bedroom. That same night, Nina helped me change the bed and rub the bloody sheets over and over in the ice-cold water we'd run into the bathtub. Every stain remover failed to live up to the task. I cried my eyes out, and Nina cried too, and when morning came, we wrung out the sheets, stuffed them into plastic bags and threw them in the bin downstairs in the courtyard.

'Come on, let's dance,' I said.

I grabbed Nina, gave her a piggyback and ran into the living room with her. But there was no one left but Herr Schlemm-Heise, who – even with the bass booming through the soles of his feet – sat snoring in his armchair. It was only one thirty-seven. Where had everyone gone?

Benno was still in the loo. He'd locked the door and as I was jiggling the handle with Nina on my back, he fended me off with a 'Just a minute!' He couldn't take his alcohol and couldn't admit it.

We found Jeff in the red salon. He'd knocked over a bottle of wine at quarter past twelve; Nina had had the presence of mind to pour a full kilo bag of salt on the stain, and that was precisely where Jeff was lying asleep. Nina knelt down in front of him.

I pulled her up off the floor, piled her onto my back again and spun her round. She squealed and shrieked, but went along with all my acrobatic attempts pliantly and pliably. I held on tight to Nina, like a figure skater holding their partner.

We left the balcony door open and the kitchen window too, so the cigarette fug could escape. Jeff hadn't moved an inch from the salt puddle. Benno was on the three-piece mattress next to him, snoring like an old man. We closed the red salon door. Herr Schlemm-Heise was still sitting in his chair, asleep. We'd clean up the next day. We climbed into the bed in Nina's room.

I had a feeling I needed to get up. My mouth and throat were parched. Ten past six. I gathered all my strength to keep my eyes open. In the bathroom, I draped myself under the tap and swallowed. The pulling sensation in my innards grew stronger. I locked the door, sat down on the toilet and kept the water running to soothe me. It hurt. I put my head on my knees and wrapped my arms around them. I was glad to be able to close my eyes again.

I didn't know how long I'd been sitting like that. I must have dozed off for a moment. Surely fifteen seconds at most. A dark lump, surrounded by a lot of blood, had come out of me. It still hurt. A beautiful pain. I took my time. When it felt safe to leave the bathroom and go to the kitchen, I turned off the tap. The kitchen was a mess and with the window open it was freezing – around minus eight degrees. I didn't feel the cold. I cleared the fifties armchair and sat down. Not even the howl of a siren could disturb the peace.

CUT

'I need to go through the score again,' Konrad says, hanging his tailcoat on the clothes rack.

'I'm going to get a glass of bubbly in the foyer,' I say, 'see you in a bit.'

'I hate premieres,' Konrad says.

'Me too.'

Konrad looks at me with sad puppy eyes. He's getting his first urge to gag. It's always the same. Nausea means he's nervous; it happens before premieres and concert tours. I stand there like a wife watching her husband gag. He's beyond help. He concentrates on not throwing up; maybe he should just do it and get it over with. But his first aid kit of Pfeffi mints and Bonaqa water is always at hand. I can go.

The ticket ladies are counting the programmes. The bar's just opened; a sparkling wine costs five marks. The tables have cards with little numbers on them. A woman with a curly hairstyle showing off the nape of her neck is eating three open sandwiches at table seven. She's chewing, her face deadly serious – she's probably a widow. Anyway, I need a drink.

Two of the Three Graces have taken up residence on the central sofa, right in the middle of the foyer. The one with the slender neck and horsy hair is the daughter, lace gloves up to her bony elbows; all in all she's probably one metre ninety. The mother is encased in a giant golden ruffle right up to her double chin, just like those fancy chocolates by the name of Rocher. She clearly likes big wrappers. She could play an Elizabethan princess in that outfit. Four black-rimmed eyes gaze over at me sorrowfully.

No one's in the smokers' area behind the glass door, just three hefty ashtrays. Not a sound gets through the glass. Everywhere I look, married couples in autumn coats are shaking hands. Husbands with partings on the left, wives with mother-of-pearl clip earrings and reddened, stretched earlobes. Married couples with an abundance of gums and polished shoes, eyeing each other up. I see you. I recognize you. Nod. See you.

On my way back to Konrad, a man with a briefcase and gelled hair rushes out of the door. 'Bleibtreu Artists' Agency, I'm an institution here,' he calls out to me, bows, can't quite straighten up properly and dashes off crookedly.

'Keep it warm for me,' Konrad says.

'What?' I ask.

Konrad shrugs and looks pale. He wants to do the rounds and see the singers, tell them to break a leg, say 'Toi toi toi' and spit over his shoulder.

'Go on then,' I say, 'I'll get another bubbly.'

We leave the room in opposite directions.

The mass of married couples has tripled. I meander through the foyer to the bar. How many glasses could I manage by seven o'clock in the worst-case scenario?

Golden Ferrero and Longneck are sitting in exactly the same pose, except that the duplicate gaze is now consumed with sadness. They've already reached the end of the line.

A half-empty glass in one hand, I go back to Konrad's room and open the door. It used to be a moment I was proud of. Only I was allowed to do that. Stage fright meets lovestruck.

'I'm looking forward to the quartet,' I say as I straighten Konrad's bow tie. I always feel the need to swallow when I see him in his finery as it looks so tight around his neck. But Konrad says he's comfortable in it.

'The tenor's lost his voice,' Konrad says, coughing and clearing his throat.

'He's just saying that,' I say.

Patent leather shoes emerge from his bag, shoe trees out, feet in, mints in trouser pocket, spare batons out of case. Glance in the mirror, kiss, glance in the mirror, kiss. Give my regards to Verdi.

As if they were threaded together, the married couples finally sit down where they belong in their season ticket seats, where they babble on with muffled voices, because they'll have to be quiet in a minute. Everything feels better now, but I didn't manage the third sparkling wine. The stalls, row five, seat three. In front of me off to one side is the widow with the curly hairstyle. She's no longer as alone as she was when she was eating her sandwiches. Curly heads with exposed napes are sitting everywhere. People crossing paths at opera premieres must cross paths at the hair stylist's too. Some local hairdresser must have had his heyday in the eighties, and hasn't changed his style since. There is not a bird's nest in sight; hairspray keeps their curls in place. Only the shape around the ears varies, but all of their ears are on display. They should be able to hear all right.

It goes dark in the auditorium. The light shines on the podium in the pit; some of it falls on the middle of the first row. Mother and daughter are sitting there, their heads turned towards the hall, their faces now overflowing with black tears. They'll never make it to the end. How did they manage to get here from the sofa anyway? And why are they sitting directly behind Konrad?

He makes his entrance: applause, a brisk bow, arms up, eye contact with trumpet and trombone players; the overture begins.

Konrad was also at the local hairdresser's. Fortunately, in the men's section, two days ago. He always gets himself shorn just before a premiere. It makes him look younger and better groomed; the old cliché of the unbridled genius is left behind on the floor.

As for me, I cut my fringe with nail scissors as soon as it starts to obstruct my view of the world. Apart from that, my hair grows and it just hangs straight: completely normal hair, actually, if only it didn't look so dull. Just this afternoon I had another try at giving it some volume with a brush and a hairdryer. But I'm so bad at holding them up and doing my hair at the same time; my arms ache and I give up before it's dry, so I hang my head down and spray an overdose of hairspray on anything that points towards the ground. When I lift my head up, my hair's standing up in all directions: it's got volume, that's for sure, but you wouldn't call it a hairstyle. It settles over the next few hours, only to end up as flat as ever. It'll probably be just like that in time for the party after the premiere.

Final chords, curtain, applause, interval. I have to bolster Konrad up with Bonaqa and compliments. I have to get a sparkling wine. I have to look in the mirror.

Konrad sits and sweats and drinks. His hair's soaking wet. He'd be good with a hairdryer: he's used to dislocating his arms at head height for hours. His gagging's over with now. It only happens before the first note sounds.

'It's going well,' I say.

'I'm good today, really good,' Konrad says.

'The tenor's great,' I say, 'he reminds me of that guy from Monty Python.'

'You mean John Cleese.'

'I'm just getting a quick glass of bubbly.'

The queue at the bar isn't long, but the bell's ringing already. The married couples are starting to thread their way back to their seats. Carrying a drink while running back to Konrad's room is just as hard as holding a hairdryer and doing your hair. Konrad's already gone. I down the glass and leave it on the floor.

Row five, seat three. I squeeze past the season ticket holders and take my seat. I've forgotten to look in the mirror. I reach up to my hair to check the volume situation and improve it. The widow in front of me off to one side is doing the same, as are probably a dozen other women behind me. We've had plenty of practice in reaching for our heads. I quickly cross my arms.

The lights go down. The two seats in the front row are empty. Just as expected: they must have gone home to take some antidepressants. They could have brought their pills with them and taken them here. Konrad makes his entrance: applause, bowing, curtain up. There's the tenor: he looks so miserable there on the red carpet, maybe he ought to start at the Ministry of Silly Walks tomorrow morning instead. Sparkling wine does perk you up. It could be that Konrad gags on behalf of all the singers; he takes on their fear of losing their voices. And it could be that on occasions like today, I have exactly the hairstyle that everyone expects from Konrad. I'll take on his hairstyle. But who will take on something of mine?

It's still got a bit of volume. Maybe I should have it layered, that would certainly help. Or a light perm, one of the gentle ones with no corrosive chemicals. Not like the one the ladies here have had. The curly hairstyle with the nape of the neck showing only bothers me because I had it myself when I was fourteen. And it wasn't just me: the whole class had the neighbourhood's universal hairstyle, even the boys. Actually, not just the whole class, it was everyone going through puberty in the whole country. The mothers protested, but they paid up the thirty marks for it, and now they've been wearing their children's collective outburst on their own heads for the last fifteen years. Maybe identity is nothing more than the communal resuscitation of a haircut from times gone by. If these women have the hairstyle they'll grow old with at the age of forty, there's hope for me yet. Babies, deaths, new jobs, divorces: every major turning point in life goes hand in hand with a new haircut. The head changes, inside and out. I really must book an appointment tomorrow.

Curtain. Wild applause. Konrad shakes hands with the first violin.

They've clearly been practising the order they bow in. The soprano brings on the directing team. It's a pity the stage director isn't wearing a toupee after all – Konrad's been fibbing to me. He has the same haircut with the left-hand parting as all the other men in the room, except that his hair has given up all resistance over the years and now forms a perfect helmet.

The married couples hurry to the cloakrooms and rush out of the theatre with their autumn coats. I've never been able to understand this head-to-head race, given the hours they're happy to spend at the opera. But the bar's nice and empty, and I get two sparkling wines, one for Konrad and one for myself, and take them back to his room.

'I was good,' Konrad says.

'Yes, you were,' I say.

Konrad just takes a sip from his glass. He'd rather have a beer. Then I'll be able to have his wine.

'Your head looked so small when you were bowing tonight.'

'You've got a screw loose,' Konrad says and puts his jeans on.

He packs up his stuff and we head off to the bar to celebrate.

The widow's sitting at table seven, eating again. When she sees Konrad, she cheerfully raises her glass of juice in his direction. Men are standing around the bar with beer and cigarettes; the chorus are looking a bit snooty in their silk shirts; the technicians have plaits down their backs. We buy beer, sparkling wine and five open sandwiches for Konrad, and sit down at table twelve.

'Wonderful, wonderful! Congratulations,' says a doe-eyed aesthete over his shoulder.

Konrad puts his half-eaten bread back on the plate, stands up, and then the theatre manager comes over and squeezes Konrad's forearm fervently, and he squeezes back. I smile; I'm still sitting down, but it doesn't matter.

The stage director arrives, and his pink and gold family of fans from the next table stand up and clap. The men pat him on the shoulder, the women kiss him and one of them highlights her admiration with a curtsy.

The theatre manager brings Konrad another beer and me another sparkling wine. I stand up. We clink our glasses.

'A wonderful evening, without a lie,' I say.

The theatre manager says he comes from Malta and he has to go back soon. I sit down again.

The Bleibtreu Artists' agent limps crookedly over to us with his briefcase. This time Konrad remains in his chair, and so do I. He's doubled over anyway.

'Wonderful, quite magical, sure to be a hit,' the agent says to Konrad.

'We know each other from somewhere,' the agent says to me.

'From earlier at the door,' I say.

'No, seriously, you're a singer.'

'Only in the bath.'

The agent's offended now and he hobbles off to table nine.

'Why don't you say what you do?' Konrad asks.

'What do I actually do?' I ask.

A woman with short hair, dyed black, sits down with Konrad and talks about the final scene's ambivalence. Her earrings are the same size as the bags under her eyes. That must be the dramaturge. I can spot them a mile off.

'I feel like an advocate for the composer,' Konrad says.

Maybe I could get some colour, a tint at least. Not black though – maybe chestnut.

The stage director has broken free from his family and wants everyone to gather around him. I get a sparkling wine, but I'm not allowed to drink it straight away. 'Working process . . . contradiction . . . inspiration . . . thank you,' the director says into the crowd, a lot of reflection and emotion in between. Not even a wind machine could move his helmet. My hair's almost certainly completely flat by now. I smile all the more steadfastly; I don't care any more. Applause. Clink, clink, clink. Cheers. There are so many beautiful hair colours out there.

That's the official part over, and now people naturally gather into groups. The stage director disappears with his fans to the café in the basement, to the cheap schnapps. Two men from the chorus play their favourite music behind the bar.

A woman with beautiful teeth and laughter lines with a man trailing behind her comes up to our table. It's the soprano. She's followed by the tenor in a hummingbird shirt, rolling his eyes, with another man trailing behind him too. A Japanese man with a Hugendubel tote bag sits down; he has the face of a cheerful child under a black mop of hair. He's the baritone. He's on his own; no relatives from the Far East tonight.

'Grazie, Maestro,' the Japanese man shouts.

'No problem, my old pal,' says Konrad and firmly hugs the baritone's shoulders. As if they've known each other for twenty years.

'It's all down to you,' says the soprano, taking Konrad's free hand between her two. She really means it. I'm not jealous at all: I've been waiting for this all evening, surprisingly. I'm neither jealous of the soprano nor proud of Konrad.

'Good material, perfect voice; shame about the syncopation,' Konrad says.

All this boss act. The way he was gagging earlier, the least he could do is thank them.

'Cheers! Hallelujah!' starts the tenor, with no inhibition whatsoever. He doesn't want to hear a thing, or see a thing: all he wants to do is sing non-stop.

'Bravissimo!' they all shout. We raise our glasses to the singers: 'Gabriela, Ralf, Teru', and then raise them the highest of all for Konrad.

'I. Am. Konrad!' Konrad says.

'To Konrad,' the others say. And the glasses clink again. They're thick as thieves. Konrad gathers up all the compliments and wants to buy a round.

'I'll get it,' I say.

At the bar, I buy beer, sparkling wine, a juice for the soprano. The tenor's sidekick helps me carry the glasses.

When I get back to the table, they're already gossiping about the stage director. That didn't take long. Konrad does a good impression of him. I go to the loo, although I'm not really sure I need to. Maybe I just need a break from smiling.

When I wash my hands, I take a look in the mirror. It's hanging there. It's hanging like a weeping willow's branches. The widow comes in, her hair flawless. Is she following me?

'So you're the conductor's wife?' she asks, a little coyly.

'Yes.'

'That's great, really great,' the widow says.

I nod and smile. 'Thank you.'

'If anyone's earned tonight's success, it's him,' she says.

Oh, so she's an expert.

'Thank you, I'll pass that on to him.'

I have to slip away, or she'll start telling me all about her life. Probably the wife of that musical director who died, or something like that.

I turn the door handle and open the stage door. It's pitch black, apart from the emergency lights shining out above the auditorium doors. I close the door behind me. Row five, seat three. The safety curtain's down. All I can see is the floor cloth across the stage and the empty orchestra pit. No more heads in sight. The two desolate Graces are unlikely to reappear. I would have bought them a drink, just to put off their suicides for a while. A few years ago, I went into the orchestra pit with Konrad after a premiere, not here but in another theatre. We screwed and fell asleep among the music stands. The cleaning lady woke us up. An empty theatre is a beautiful thing.

Konrad comes down the aisle towards me.

'I was looking for you,' he says.

Konrad's glad to have found me. He sways a little as he's standing in front of me.

'You know, Konrad,' I say.

'What?' he asks.

'I have to go to the hairdresser.'

'If you say so.'

'All off, I'll get it all chopped off.'

'Do it.'

He stifles a yawn.

'Shall we?' he asks.

'Just one more for the road,' I say.

BACK ON SPEAKING TERMS

I arrive at the Ostbahnhof three hours in advance. I came on an earlier train just to be on the safe side. I take a taxi. I don't want to have to rush, not for anything in the world. And I want to be the first one there, to see the cemetery on my own, before anyone else shows up.

'To Pankow, please,' I say.

I spot my father standing at the Jannowitz Bridge crossing, among all the other pedestrians waiting for the light to turn green. I duck down in the back seat. We pass by very close to him. I turn around. The pedestrians set off across the road, my father first of all. But it's not him. My father has a different walk. The taxi driver eyes me in the mirror.

I get out at Wollankstrasse. I can walk the last few steps. The park is quiet, under the May sun. It's well looked after, but not over-manicured. The paths twist and turn; there's no end in sight. There are shadows. I'm shocked when I suddenly realize I've been missing the sun all these months; Karl's managed to pick one of those rare days when the spring summons up the strength to look like summer. I was right to put on sandals and ditch the tights for the first time this year before the dew had even dried this morning. Bare feet, garnet-red hair and a denim jacket, that's what I'm wearing for Karl. I take off the jacket and tie it around my hips.

The cemetery unfolds imperceptibly from the park; it's grown into it, protected by it, so it remains hidden from anyone who doesn't know the area, and yet it's exactly where I remember it. I walk up to the brick wall, barely visible under moss and weeds. There's no gate, just two decrepit pillars, covered by the limp branches of young birch trees randomly multiplying.

I enter. The cemetery is old, weathered, grandiose. No wonder Karl chose this one. We came here several times, back then, ten years ago. Karl wouldn't have stopped walking through the cemetery just because I left him. He moved here to Pankow so his walks would be nicer. In the breaks between the morning and evening rehearsals, he'd tread the paths in the park day after day until he knew all the trees by name, every inch of the place, every view. Away from the din of the city, Karl began to feel at home in Berlin.

I picture him now: sitting down here on a stone and smoking two or three cigarettes, among the old family tombs, in the midst of the wild undergrowth, his gaze wandering along the ivy-clad trunks and up into the tree-tops forming a canopy. If he has neither rehearsals nor any idea if he's needed at the theatre, his walks will be longer. He'll sit still on the stone, not moving until he's spotted a hare nibbling on something or until he thinks he can hear a hedgehog rustling in the decaying heaps of leaves. Karl might lose all sense of time. He'll only notice how long he's been here from the pile of fag ends he'll nudge against the stone with his toe. Karl stands up, runs his hand through his hair and thinks he ought to talk to Franz again. He has to talk to Franz again so it can go back to the way it used to be, back in the good old days. Karl can't believe there isn't a place for him in Franz's razor-sharp, potent version of theatre. Karl can't stand it. That's why he has to talk to Franz again. Karl goes home, climbs the five flights of stairs to his attic, takes the bottle of Berentzen from the fridge and drinks his first schnapps of the day. If Karl doesn't have a performance, there's no reason to stay sober. He sits down at the kitchen table, quiet as the grave. Karl empties half the bottle; it takes him from early evening to midnight. Karl knows better than most how to forget time. He doesn't have a watch, and neither do I.

I get up and walk over to a man in green dungarees trying to tame the bushes with some shears.

'Do you have the time?' I ask.

'Half past one,' the man says.

'But there's a funeral here at two o'clock, right?' I ask.

'There haven't been any funerals here for years, you can see that,' the man says without looking up from his snipping.

'So where's the Bürgerpark cemetery?' I ask.

Now he lowers his shears and shows me where to go with an outstretched arm.

'Ten, fifteen minutes from here,' he says, pursing his lips disparagingly.

People who can't just give you a little encouragement make me want to scream. I start running, through the park, over the bridge, past the fountain on the right.

I've been away from Berlin for too long; there's no denying it. I've got my cemeteries mixed up. Once I'm past the playground on the left, I can see the fence, endlessly long and freshly painted, surrounding the Bürgerpark cemetery. I need to follow it all the way to the front, then turn to reach the main entrance.

This isn't a cemetery; it's a fenced-off rectangle with plots, allotments; it's a trailer park, an open-air barracks. But what's Karl doing here? Before I reach the corner where a gravestone business is displaying its wares, I slow down and put on my denim jacket. I turn right. That must be the entrance up ahead, where all the cars are parked.

I'm walking on pale grey concrete alongside the fence. I pass street lights, their regularity reminding me that my destination's inevitably drawing closer. I can see people standing in small groups in front of the gate; some are looking in my direction. The concrete turns into cotton wool. But my fence and street lamp allies keep me on track.

I recognize all of them straight away from afar, without a moment's doubt. They weren't expecting me. Don't rush, don't dawdle, don't trip over. Just walk normally, head held high if you can. They know exactly who I am. But after ten years, they can safely pretend they can't remember me. My feet have become mechanical walking contraptions, eating away at cotton wool by the metre. Don't wimp out now. Go, damn it. The young women are huddled together, scuffing the concrete with their shoes: Anja Haberfeld, Annett Henicke and Carolin Rönn, their children all with one and the same father – Franz. Franz isn't there yet. Franz is the theatre manager. He arrives at the last minute, with Gerry, who plays the leading roles for him. It's Gerry who plays them, not Karl.

The street lights glide past me, one after the other. Don't go off course. No funny business. Walk up to the people you know, the ones who know you, whether they like it or not. Karl can't take you by the hand any more, you're really too old for that. I stomp through the cotton wool, short of breath, shaky, my teeth clenched. Don't do things by halves now. Let's do this. Eyes open. Head up. Catch someone's eye. You know actors can't ever come up and say hello, for one simple reason: they don't want to see – they want to be seen. You have to go straight into the midst of them. Into the pack of actors. Deep breath. I let out a much too quiet, whimpering 'Hello' and a completely insignificant 'Afternoon'. The corners of my mouth are twitching. Twice I give a nod with my head: brief, scant, tiny movements. No reaction. I remember the hundreds of evenings when I put myself through a test of courage just to enter the canteen alone to wait for Karl, walking past the full, noisy actors' tables, wilting under imagined glances that never materialized, panicking as I searched for somewhere safe to sit, somewhere that didn't exist without Karl. Now I see that all those evenings were nothing but long-planned practice for today – for the moment I'd come to a halt in the midst of a crowd of actors who'd aged by ten years. I'm one of them; I'm one of Karl's colleagues.

I can feel their eyes on me. They're so bad at being inconspicuous. What did Karl tell them? What could be rattling through their brains at the sight of me? I'm not moving from this spot. I listen to their babbling, whispering, giggling; I see the kisses they're exchanging when they see each other, the cigarettes they're lighting, the flowers they've brought. I came without flowers on my long journey, no troublesome props; I had enough trouble getting myself here. Karl's colleagues aren't lowering their voices, nor are they in black. They're just muffling their excitability until this is over. And by their standards, they're looking colourful, lightly dressed, maybe because the sun's out and they witness it so rarely. They're getting an extra helping of daylight, as they can leave the theatre earlier than usual today. Rehearsals finished at one o'clock: they've got Karl to bury.

Karl will forever be in blue, denim blue. Jeans, denim jacket, denim shirt. And Karl just has two seasons: in the winter he wears trainers, in the summer Jesus creepers – that's the only difference. When Karl's decided it's summer, he takes off his socks in relief and steps into his sandals, even if his feet might freeze.

'Hi, Tanja.'

We set eyes on each other, hug, walk away. Ute Schmitt has been playing a kind-hearted nurse in a TV series for a few years now because Franz stopped giving her any roles. Karl can't bear her; she leaves her inner do-gooder hanging out, he says. Karl can't stand women of his own age in any case. A compassionate mother like her is just what I need right now. I'll take the TV nurse's kindness at face value. She looks concerned, I look grateful. Karl can't see us anyway.

Karl's daughter Fine walks up to the entrance. She's wearing a knee-length black coat and sunglasses and she's holding a yellow rose. Fine is the same age as me. We liked each other, even then. Fine had to hand Karl, her father, over to me when we were both eighteen. If Fine hadn't been Karl's daughter and I hadn't been Karl's lover, we could have become friends. When I left Karl, Fine and I lost touch with each other too. I got her number from directory enquiries just four weeks ago. Since then, we've often talked on the phone, for hours, our voices thin. We've talked about Karl.

Fine presses her hot cheek to mine. I'd forgotten she was a whole head taller than me. She's overcome and starts to cry. She's slimmed down and become even more beautiful. Tears are streaming under her sunglasses. I try to look her in the eye, but in the lenses of her glasses all I can make out is my own face, twice.

'I have no idea how this is going to go,' Fine says, sniffling. Protected by her sunglasses, she tries to get her bearings and work out who's with whom; it's hopeless, so she looks down and smooths her coat with an unsteady hand. I give her a Tempo tissue.

Franz and Gerry appear, slamming their car doors. They rush over, their faces stony and their jackets flapping open.

Gerry mingles; Franz walks past all of us, scarcely glancing at anyone, his lips thin, his skin pale, his short-sighted grey eyes scurrying back and forth behind his metal-framed glasses. When he's bothered by something, Franz can look terrible: grumpy, humourless, cynical. That's when Karl calls him Spitzweg, after the painter, and Franz answers back, 'Well, well, Fred Flintstone's woken up!' It's only Gerry, vain, stingy, good with dogs, who's never really earned a nickname.

Franz dashes into the cemetery through the gate and disappears into the quaint little red-brick chapel. Has he been here before? How does he know what he's got to do?

It was for Franz that Karl left Dresden, where he'd been on stage for fifteen years. He went to Berlin to open a new theatre with Franz, which went on to be a roaring success. I see Karl again as he was: always afraid of this city, where they're starting to replace all the walls with panes of glass. Karl prefers to sit in the canteen. He thinks he's safe there. I skulk around the theatre, always on the lookout for a hiding place. Karl sees. He sees me long before I see him. Through the canteen's basement windows, Karl can see my legs going up and down the stairs night after night. On one of these nights he beckons me over. Karl gathers me up. Karl lets me in. Karl takes me with him. He takes me to his cockroach-infested Plattenbau apartment and we play games; we have all the fun my father promised me all my life but never had in him; we have the fun Fine will have to forego for ever from now on.

Franz sticks his head out of the chapel door and twitches

involuntarily; he has assumed a habit of bobbing his head frantically, as if he were constantly trying to shake something off.

'Let's go,' he says softly.

It doesn't seem appropriate for a solemn funeral; it sounds like he's calling for a quick run-through. The horde lazily gathers and heads to the chapel. It takes me along with it, and I let myself be carried. We squeeze through the door Franz has opened. The chapel is small and has a musty smell. There is no chance of us all fitting in. At the front there's a pulpit: a chunky wooden box with a tiny dome over it. Without a second thought, I sit down in the penultimate row, at the very end. The penultimate row. I've always liked that spot, even in the theatre, although there isn't a single logical reason for it. The wooden pews are filled in no time. The actors are densely packed in the central aisle, against the whitewashed wall at the back, at the sides, in the chapel door. Most of the bunch have to stay outside, hanging out of the chapel like the fat rear end of a bee. Karl's funeral is hopelessly sold out.

Old Rothert and his lady friend Susanne are sitting on my left. On my right are Wagner, Althaus and Meyer. The hulking Mattuschek and tall Böhm are in front of me. I probably won't see much, in a lousy seat, hemmed in by Karl's colleagues. But more than anything, I won't be able to see because sad music starts playing from a tape somewhere which promptly, much as I fight it, brings tears to my eyes, obscures my vision and makes my temples throb. I lower my head, let my hair hang in front of my face, rummage for the tissues. The crowd sits, stands, waits, silent and motionless. The murmuring and whispering has stopped. Just this music. Time stands still. Why did they pick something classical anyway? Karl never listens to classical music. Karl's favourites are 'Twist in My Sobriety' by Tanita Tikaram and 'Hope of Deliverance' by Paul McCartney. And Elvis, of course, that's what he grew up with.

After an eternity, Franz steps up to the pulpit. The music fades out. His head jerks. He swallows. His Adam's apple slips up and down his spindly neck under his large-pored skin. The room swallows along with him. Franz begins to speak, much too quietly, much too slowly, without any sense of addressing the crowd. He starts so low, weary and ill-tempered that it's embarrassing. But appearances are deceptive. Franz has sneakily learned to slow his blood pressure so he can preserve his energy. Once he's warmed up, he can carry on talking for hours, firing out his boiled-down thoughts, making everyone's ears prickle and brains glow, until we all come to admire him – Karl and I and all the others. It's just that at first it doesn't look like this bumbling intellectual has a plan at all. But he always has one, you can rely on that.

Franz pulls out a well-worn textbook: Heiner Müller, *The Construction Site*. He speaks of the beginning of a friendship: the friendship between him and Karl which began in Dresden in the mid-eighties. Their performances all sold out, and people came from Berlin and all around, and climbed through the toilet windows in a frenzy to get inside the theatre to see Franz's productions with Karl as the lead. Franz reads aloud Karl's lines as Brigadier Barka, and then the one line, Karl's line as only he could deliver it, the Heiner Müller line made legendary by Karl, a milestone in Franz's career: 'I am the ferry between the Ice Age and the commune.'

Franz tilts his head upwards, his gaze goes up into the void, into the dome, inwards; his crisply defined dot eyes are nimble, and he looks even thinner behind the pulpit, like a dishevelled, starved city pigeon. He talks about Karl's power on stage, about his beefy, proletarian physical presence that could, and would, roar, and that delivered the most philosophical sentences as if they were lullabies: simple, naïve, gentle. Karl sits on the empty stage like a stubborn child; Brigadier Barka has drunk the prize away, Gerry stands behind him with the accordion, the stage begins to turn, Karl agonizes, raises his fist, Gerry plays him a song, 'Brothers, to the Sun, to Freedom', the country's dissolving from within, the bittersweet dream is over and the stage keeps turning, Karl sings, but his tears of rage drown out the song. Only Karl can do that. Only Karl can get away with it. If Franz were to flap up to the edge of the pulpit, stir up the dust and lose a few stuck-together feathers, we'd be able to see the crippled pigeon's feet clawing around on the wood.

Franz doesn't say that Karl sits at the canteen table all night long, drinking beer and schnapps with his shirt sleeves rolled up, resting his elbows on the wood, pulling his hair out, firing up the world with his convictions, laughing, crying, swearing, shifting between rage and melancholy. Franz doesn't say that Karl has practically no neck at all, that Karl can't dry his own back, that Karl showed me what the word 'fuck' meant. Franz doesn't say that Karl slammed his forehead into the glass door of the Düsseldorf hotel breakfast room, and that the guests stopped eating and stared at Karl as if he was too stupid to walk through a door.

Franz certainly doesn't say that Karl, deep down, is Lotti, the sweet but simple hippopotamus, off on all kinds of adventures with me, the nimble, sly cat Miaow, defeating every foe and scratching her back on my claws at night and rubbing her belly against my fur. The saleswoman in the ladies' department thought we were being childish when, after she'd asked Karl what Dad wanted to buy for his daughter, I replied saying he wasn't my Dad, this was Lotti and she needed a new skirt. Karl vehemently and belatedly showed me how to be a child. I want to appeal to all the fathers of the world, to ask them to regularly and unrestrainedly play at being animals for their daughters: horses, bears, monkeys, whatever comes to mind – lions, pigs or elephants. If they don't, they'll be punished with sons-in-law older than themselves who'll mess up all the family photos with their huge nostrils and square heads. My appeal will come too late for my own father. My father isn't an animal and won't ever become one; he doesn't have a hint of animal in him – this is something I've known for a long time. My father spent my entire childhood trying to prevent the Third World War. As a peace-keeping military spy, he can't be an animal: if he were, all the enemy would have to do was lure him in with the right food, and my father would be tamed and eat out of their hands.

Franz was with Karl in the hospital, a few days before he died. They talked, Franz says, twisting his pigeon's head at an even sharper angle upwards, and as they talked at his bedside, they came to terms with some of the things that had driven them apart over recent years. Why they had to go their separate ways. Why their friendship was over. Franz takes a breath. The pigeon ought to coo at this point. It doesn't though – after all, Franz is a professional. He carries on talking, his eyes clearly fixed on the room. When Franz turned around again as he was leaving, Karl had a strange look in his eyes, as if something very important remained unfinished. Franz says it as it is. As simple as that. And he tells us to our faces what he couldn't say to Karl: cheer up, old man, it's going to be OK.

The pigeon hangs on in there; it sizes up the room and looks pitiful. Franz is searching for his crowd's eyes. They faithfully return his gaze. And suddenly, Franz is gone; the bird's fallen from its perch. We look at the empty pulpit and hear, first, the echo of a click, then a hiss from under the dome. Franz reappears. He was pressing the Play button on a cassette recorder, which appears to be on the floor behind the pulpit.

Goodnight, my friends,
It's time for me to go.
All that I haven't said,
Takes one last cigarette
And just one more for the road.

My feet are freezing. The tissues are all used up and sodden. Karl, I know why Franz couldn't give you roles any more. He couldn't bear the fact that you cry sometimes.

We get up and stand there. For a moment. One more moment. And another. Then the horde moves back out into the open. As we step through the door we're blinded by the sun. The actors form a queue, headed up by Franz and the family, as naturally as if they'd done nothing but attend funerals all their lives. The crowd that had to stay outside earlier is forced to wait again and becomes the snake's tail this time. Detlef from props and Olli from sound go in front of me. Behind me are Veronika Fleischer and Bruni Dittmanns, the director's secretaries. I'm walking alone, perhaps the only one in this endless, sad kindergarten class lined up two by two. Just as I loved Karl on my own and left him on my own, I also want to bury him on my own. In each hand I'm holding three softened tissues shrivelled from moisture, alternating between them to wipe my nose. I look down at my frozen feet, which look utterly purple in their sandals. The sand we're walking over is slightly damp. With every step, the toes of my shoes throw some of it into the air. With every step, I tread on my predecessors' footprints, leaving mine behind for a moment, only to be replaced by the next in line with their own. The good thing about sandals is that the sand that gets in at the front falls out at the back. Next to my feet, a pair of dark brown men's shoes appears, the kind they call slip-ons, with woven leather uppers. I lower my head: I don't want a sidekick, a hanger-on or an ally of convenience for the occasion. Out of the corner of my eye, I can see that there are feet in pale socks in the shoes; the dark green trousers with the crease ironed in are a little too short. I know that walk. I know it very well, this walk with the toes pointing slightly outwards, inconspicuous and precise. For a fraction of a second, my eyes shoot up the trouser seam to the hem of the leather jacket. It's him. I hide behind my hair, burying my face into my tissue-crumpling hands. This man is my father. I haven't seen him for an eternity. The blood's boiling in my temples. If he speaks to me now, I'll scream. I can feel an artery throbbing in my neck. If he touches me now, I'll erupt. What's that fucking snoop doing here? My eyes are popping out of my head; my feet are melting into the sand. Stay away from me, you snitch. There's a furious thumping in my ears. I can't breathe. All the exits are blocked. Get lost. Go away, or I'll snap, and there'll be blood. How dare you interfere with my funeral? Go. Leave me alone. I'm about to explode. He's not going away. He won't leave me alone. Water streams forth out of me. Not just from my eyes, no, it's pouring off me from all over. My entire head's weeping, my forehead's swimming, my scalp's dripping. It runs down on me, washes the colour out of my hair, my tears are turning garnet-red, drawing tracks over my skin, bloody lines are creeping down my body, winding over my neck, chest and back, drops are falling on my bare feet, I'm dragging a train of wet red threads behind me, slowly congealing and clumping somewhere in the sand. Have you been secretly watching me, lurking in the bushes, getting 'intel', as you call it, making sure you're never seen yourself? That's what spies do, even when they furtively go to funerals that belong to their daughters' past loves. Why won't you leave me in peace?

He prowls alongside me, without a glance, without a word, without a sound. He doesn't say a thing. He has no intention of saying anything, or he would have done so by now. He's on the right, I'm on the left; an invisible wall hangs between us. What more could there be to say now? You're no help, you're a fucking burden to me, Dad. You could have helped me, but you didn't. You didn't tell me Karl was dying. But you know everything. You knew and you didn't tell me. This is how you punish me for never wanting to see you again. It's easy for a spy like you, obtaining information and deliberately withholding it, as soon as you're deprived of something. But I'm not your go-between, Dad, you have to get it into your head: you're not my commanding officer.

The streams of water are petering out. I'm beginning to dry up, struggling with involuntary twitches, using all my might to suppress the sobs racing out of my heart unannounced. With stoic perseverance, the line of people crawls across the sand. The funeral procession doesn't take the shortest but the most convoluted, the most protracted, the most complicated path; we cautiously circle Karl's final resting place – we're putting off the conclusion. I don't know if I'll last to the end. I'll never find the way back again. My father's walking by my side without me asking him to. I didn't ask anyone to, least of all him. I don't want special treatment, not any more. But you should have told me Karl was dying, Dad.

I found out about it from the paper, like everyone else going through the culture pages. I saw the little announcement: it said 'after a short, serious illness'. I quickly shut the paper then opened it again. It was still there. I called the theatre and asked if it was true. Then I went for a run through the forest. For two hours I panted, spluttered and coughed my lungs up. I knew straight away it was lung cancer. Fine confirmed it later on the phone. The day I found out Karl died coincided with my personal best. After four years of abstinence, I bought myself a pack of cigarettes, Lord Extras. Within two weeks, I was back to forty a day. I'll keep smoking for you, Karl, one after another; I'll smoke forty cigarettes, Dad, those harmful, expensive things you confiscated, threw down the toilet, chopped up with your scissors one by one before my eyes. I'll never tire of sending you smoke signals.

The tissues in my hands are starting to fall apart. My father doesn't try to look at me, establish contact with me, catch a secret sign from me. He's making no demands. He ambushed me from behind so he wouldn't ask anything of me. First shock, then relief. I look at his feet, which are walking at the same rhythm as mine. Same pace. There must be lots of sand in his shoes from walking to Karl's grave. He'll take off his slip-ons tonight, rip off his socks and shake out the sand he took home from the cemetery. He'll be amazed how much there is. But no one will find out about it. All he'll have to do is get rid of the sand. With the dustpan or the hoover.

Our pace slows down, falters. The funeral procession

comes to a halt and bunches up again. Without me knowing how or where, my father's gone. He's left me standing there, and I'm not looking for him. So that was that. That was what he'd had in mind for me, against my will, without asking for my consent. I don't know what he's up to, but I'm sure he won't wait till the end. Arriving late and leaving early: it's almost as if you hadn't been there.

The place by my side is taken by someone else; it's Beppo, the chef from the canteen. We gather on the edge of a patch of grass in the shadow of some lanky pines, birches and poplars. This is where the fresh graves are, where the recent dead are lying. The grass is only here on a temporary basis: soon it will be covered with new rows of graves. I can see Fine walking alone across it; she's stepping through the long grass. She's holding a wreath. She places it in the middle of the first row, between a hole dug in the ground and the molehill resulting from it. This is Karl's space. A tiny building site. It's cramped between the other graves, each measuring just one square metre, with no gaps between them. But Karl's claustrophobic. Fine stands back up. Her lips are moving. Then she takes the yellow rose from her coat pocket and bends down again to place it in front of the hole. Fine reaches into the waist-high bowl on a pedestal, which looks like the round ashtrays you find by every stage door, the ones they use to wedge the door open to let a little air into the theatre in the summer. She takes a handful of earth and lets it trickle into the hole. Then she turns around and walks across the grass to the other side.

Franz makes his way to Karl, throws him a few crumbs of earth like birdseed and stalks away on his skinny legs. Gerry does the same, chewing gum as he goes. Then it's the turn of the boys from the technical department: Kalle, Hansi, Frosch, Ecki. It takes courage to take your time, knowing everyone is watching you as you go, as you take the earth and scatter it, as you stand, as you walk away. My father does it all just as he saw the others doing it, only a little more diffidently. He has the ugliest bouquet of all: pink, purple and white dwarf chrysanthemums with layers and layers of metallic cellophane and black ribbons all around them. My father looks small, almost bent over, and probably later on, when I have the strength to see him again, he'll have become even smaller and even more bent over. I snatched my wrist, the wrist of a child, from an officer's firm, pinching grasp and laid my head in the lap of a drunkard lulling me to sleep. The drunkard is dead. My father's done. He brushes the remains of the earth off his fingers, walks over to the group opposite and disappears into it. Now he can get lost; now he can run away through the bushes he emerged from. No fuss, no noise, no traces, no witnesses. Appeared out of the blue, swallowed up off the face of the earth. No one will know he was with me when we buried Karl.

I'm standing next to Ute Schmitt, the TV nurse. It's almost our turn. I stuff the tissues, by now combined into a mass of fibre, into my denim jacket's inside pocket. Ute Schmitt takes my hand and gives me one of her warm TV looks.

'Who's going first?' she asks.

'Me,' I say.

The grass is wet; I don't notice until I've started walking. I've got cold, wet feet in sandals and no more tissues. A strip of grass has been trampled by those who went before me. I follow in their footsteps. In front of the grave there's a semicircular patch of flattened earth and blades of grass lying in a jumbled pattern as if slaughtered, no longer able to stand up. I step up to it and look into the hole. An urn no bigger than a beach bucket, with earth crumbled over it: as if children had started building something and then lost interest halfway through. How could you let yourself be defeated like this, Karl? Didn't you fight back at all? Why didn't you go to the doctor until you were less than seventy kilos and spitting up blood? You didn't fight back one bit, you coward. The same with Franz: you never talked to him; all you ever did was talk about how you needed to talk to him again. You're so weak in that beefy body of yours. Every evening you decide you have to talk to Franz all over again, over your schnapps glass. You're such a stupid man. I'm going. I can't listen to it any more. I'm so tired of hearing it. Late at night, when even the last down-and-out has left you sitting there, you stagger home, your eyes leaking and your shoelaces undone. But when you're tanked up you can't find the keyhole. You spend the night on the doormat in front of your apartment. At some point I wake up and pick you up from the doormat. You look like a toad, with that torpor in your face, with those crude, distorted expressions in slow motion. You pee next to the toilet bowl and fall into bed. I pull the clothes off you. You're nothing more than a snoring mountain of flesh. You make me want to puke, Karl Kreuschler. You don't talk to Franz, not one single bloody time. I'll tell you why: because if you did, you'd be out on your ear, at best. You should be glad Franz still pays you enough to cover your bottles of Berentzen and your packets of Lord Extras. You cut a laughable figure, Karl, an old soak masquerading as a revolutionary; a bad, has-been canteen clown blowing a bit of hot air when you've got a schnapps glass in front of you. You've pickled your brains, you idiot. That's why Franz doesn't cast you any more. Go on, cry – it's only schnapps pouring out of your eyes. That's not what I ran away from home for when I was eighteen, do you get it now? You lied to me, told me terrible lies, lied to me and lied to everyone, and most of all you lied to yourself. You're not in the old overgrown cemetery where we used to walk, and you never went there again, not once. The only one who went there was me, what a fool. Because of you, I went to the wrong cemetery. But you're buried in the tiniest of plots, in locker number one hundred and thirty-four, and do you know what your neighbour's name is, Karl? No one would believe you anyway; your neighbour's name is Lothar Schnapps, it's engraved there on the stone. He died six weeks before you, and the flowers on his grave have already withered. Farewell, Karl. Adieu, Lotti.

I walk over to the other side. My nose is running. No tissues. I'll have to use my sleeve. I've been completely drained. I stand in the crowd, next to the guys from the technical department.

I can hear them whispering: here and there soft words are being spoken, mumbled, directed to the ground. The faces are brightening. The actors are already setting off, just pausing for a moment, out of politeness. Finally it's Sabine, the prompter's, turn. She places a bunch of tulips on top of the mountain of flowers. She comes over to us. We're all here, except Karl. Karl would be glad he didn't have to be here. He would have had to go an eternity without a smoke.

Franz leaves, followed by Gerry. The horde trots behind in small disorderly groups. We steer clear of the grass; no one wants to walk on it. The chattering and whispering starts again. Cautiously at first, then it swells; as the distance from Karl's grave increases, the volume goes up. Peschke tells me they're thinking of running his play in Tübingen.

'Still the same old one, the one about the pilot with a fear of flying?' I ask.

'Yes, that's the one,' Peschke says.

He doesn't get to write much these days, what with the children and all that. He puts a cigarette in the corner of his mouth. Through rows of graves, past hedges, over sand and gravel paths, we head back to the chapel, along other paths, across other grassy patches. There are no rules when it comes to leaving. I'd have trouble finding my way out of here on my own, but I'm in safe hands in the herd taking me to the exit. The way back is a piece of cake; it takes a fraction of the time it took us to get there. Outside the cemetery gate, the lighters click, the cigarettes glow and we take a deep breath. They are hard-earned rewards, inhaled with greed and relish, the smoke pushing the actors' mouths skywards.

Fine comes over to me.

'Now we've found each other again,' she says, 'maybe we could see each other more often.' We look at one another and can't help but grin at each other's sore and cried-out eyes. We look like two barn owls with the flu.

The horde dissipates, breaking apart in all directions. The hugs are all done, meetings are arranged at the top of their voices, car doors are slammed. They rush off, full steam ahead to the theatre, to the canteen, where Franz has had a buffet laid out. There's no more work today – just drinking. I don't drink schnapps any more; I don't like it, but sometimes I'll have one anyway, for Karl.

I start walking, alongside the fence, past the street lights. The sun's reflecting on the concrete. I don't know what time it is. At the corner with the gravestone business, I take my denim jacket off and tie it around my hips. I pass the playground, the fountain, and cross the bridge. I light another cigarette. It's peaceful in the park. I probably won't visit the old cemetery again, much as I'd like to now. I cross Wollankstrasse and get caught up in the hustle and bustle of the shoppers, the rush hour traffic, the usual commotion going on in Pankow in the afternoon. I can feel my feet thawing out. I can see floral dresses, mobile phones, bare calves, plastic carrier bags. Very slowly, life returns to my feet. But I can't pick up the rhythm of the city. It simply isn't possible to go any faster. I see cars squeezing into spaces and children running after the tram. I'm going to miss my train. That's not so bad. I'll take the next one, or the one after that. People jostle me; I don't mind. The blood's well and truly come back to my feet now. I've found my walking pace. I move slowly and steadily through Berlin. I'm not taking a taxi. I'm walking. I'm going. From Pankow to the Ostbahnhof, on foot.

KATJA OSKAMP was born in 1970 in Leipzig and grew up in Berlin. She began her career in the theatre as a playwright and went on to study at the German Literature Institute in Leipzig. She is the author of five books: *Half Swimmer* (2003), *The Dust Collector* (2007), *Hellersdorfer Pearl* (2010), *Marzahn, Mon Amour* (2019), and *The Penultimate Woman* (2024). *Marzahn, Mon Amour* won the Dublin Literary Award in 2023.

JO HEINRICH is a translator from German and French. Her translation of Katja Oskamp's *Marzahn, Mon Amour* was awarded the Dublin Literary Award, and was shortlisted for the Warwick Prize for Women in Translation and the TA First Translation Prize. Other recent translations include *The Invention of Good and Evil* by Hanno Sauer (Profile Books, 2024).

THE PEIRENE SUBSCRIPTION

Since 2011, Peirene Press has run a subscription service which has brought a world of translated literature to thousands of readers. We seek out great stories and original writing from across the globe, and work with the best translators to bring these books into English – before sending each one to our subscribers ahead of publication. All of our books are beautifully designed collectible paperback editions, printed in the UK using sustainable materials.

Join our reading community today and subscribe to receive three or six books a year, as well as invitations to events and launch parties and discounts on all our titles. We also offer a gift subscription, so you can share your literary discoveries with friends and family.

A one-year subscription costs £38 for three books, or £68 for six books, including UK shipping. International postage costs apply.

www.peirenepress.com/subscribe

'The foreign literature specialist'

The Sunday Times

'A class act'

The Guardian